LIBRA

EDITED BY AUSTIN P. SHEEHAN
& HELENA MCAULEY

THE ZODIAC SERIES

The Zodiac Series is a collection of twelve speculative fiction anthologies, each focusing on one of the Zodiac signs. The anthologies feature short stories and poems inspired by each sign, and retellings of the various myths behind those signs.

\#

Capricorn Aquarius Pisces

Aries Taurus Gemini

Cancer Leo Virgo

Libra Scorpio Sagittarius

\#

The Zodiac Series has been produced by Aussie Speculative Fiction, and each anthology contains a diverse selection of tales by talented writers from Australia and New Zealand.

I AM LIBRA

Zoey Xolton

I am the Scales and my constellation is Libra.

My tarot card is Justice; I am a peace-keeper and am socially
minded.

At my best I am cooperative, diplomatic and gracious.

At my worst I am indecisive, self-pitying and bitter.

Intellectual and free, like my element: Air, mine is a Cardinal sign.

I appreciate harmony, sharing, gentleness and time outdoors.

However, I dislike conformity, violence and injustice.

I am ruled by Venus, and am guardian to the fifth day of the week.

My colours are pink and green.

About the Author:

Zoey Xolton is an Australian Speculative Fiction writer, primarily of Dark Fantasy, Paranormal Romance, and Horror. Her works have appeared in over one-hundred themed anthologies, with more due for publication!

She has recently celebrated the release of her debut short story collection Darkly Ever After. *You can find further details regarding her many publications on her website:* www.zoeyxolton.com*!*

CONTENTS:

FOREWORD

Sasha Hanton

Represented by a set of scales, which once were considered the claws of Scorpio, Libra is the youngest of the Zodiac signs. Ruled over by the planet Venus, the seventh sign of the zodiac is the only one not represented by an animal or human.

Looking into the history of Libra you will find that the constellation was only catalogued by the Romans approximately 3,500 years ago, they divided the claws from Scorpio to create their Libra which incorporated the Autumnal Equinox and the balance between day and night. Whilst the current designation of Libra was done by the Romans, they were not the first to separate the stars into a constellation; the Babylonians had a name for them which translated to "the heavenly weighing scales". However, the ancient Greeks knew the constellation as Chelae or "claws" and considered it the claws of Scorpio; though when the Romans dubbed them Libra the sign became associated with the Greek

Goddess Astraea, and other goddesses of Justice. Libra still bears a connection to when it was the claws of Scorpio with its two brightest stars Zubeneschamali and Zubenelgenubi, respectively meaning "Northern Claw" and "Southern Claw" in Arabic.

The myth most associated with Libra is also linked to Virgo; it is the myth of the goddess Astraea. Daughter of Zeus and Themis (in some accounts there is debate on who her parents are), Astraea is said to be the last of the gods to live on Earth with humankind. She watched humanity become sinful and, deeming them as no longer upholding justice, she decided to leave the Earth and rose up into the skies becoming the constellation of Virgo while her scales of justice became the constellation of Libra.

Coming from its connection to a goddess of Justice it is no wonder that the constellation shares a special tie to the Justice, eleventh card of the Major Arcana of the Tarot. Adorned with a seated figure holding a double-edged sword in her right hand and a scale in her left, this card has a clear meaning: balance. Finer details in the imagery often show the figure seated between two pillars, a single jewel in her crown, and perhaps most significant of all the lack of a blindfold—symbolising that the figure is a personification of spiritual justice. However, the Justice card also stands for injustice, inequality and chaos when in reverse. In relation to Libra the card represents the poised and balanced nature most Libras possess along with keen intuition but can also be said to show in reverse the risks a Libra can face at becoming unbalanced.

FOREWORD

Aside from being well balanced, organised, and capable decision makers, Libra natives are known for being charming which is no surprise with their ruling planet being Venus. Named after the Roman counterpart to Aphrodite, the Greek Goddess of love and beauty, Venus bestows those under its rule with beauty, charm, a cheerful demeanour, and a leaning towards the arts and other creative fields. However, the planet also imbues them with a love for finer things, a craving for company, and a vulnerability towards becoming careless or lazy. Libras tend to share similar traits with Taurus natives thanks to their shared ruling planet of Venus, though they don't share all their traits.

For those born between September 23rd and October 22nd Libra grants its gifts. An upstanding drive for justice or a desire for harmony may guide a Libra's hand. As you flip through the pages of this anthology prepare to see not only harmony and balance but undoubtedly the chaos that can unfold when the scales tip, revealing what lurks beneath waiting for Libra to lose its path.

About the Author:

Sasha Hanton grew up in the tropics of Darwin, Northern Territory. From a young age, she devoured books and iced coffee, both of which she continues to intake on an almost daily basis. Now living on beautiful Bribie Island in Queensland, her time is split between writing and spoiling her puppy Miley.

Sasha, who has a Bachelor of Journalism from Bond University, has dabbled in the journalistic profession but finds fiction far more fascinating. Her first published work The Short Story Press Collection *draws on her love for a diverse range of genres and passion for short stories. Coming from a multicultural background (Eurasian) she aspires to make her writing inclusive for people from all walks of life and to bring a unique blend of eastern and western culture to her writing.*

Throughout her life, she has been a lover of history and mythology, and at any time will find some way to worm one or the other into her storytelling. When she's not writing or reading she can be found walking her dog and volunteering. You can keep up with her writing over on www.theshortstorypress.wordpress.com

THE SCALES ALWAYS BALANCE

LJ McLeod

"The scales always balance." My grandfather always said that, even before the Alzheimer's. I thought it was the Russian equivalent of "Karma's a bitch". That is, until the day he grabbed my wrist, looked me right in the eye and said, "The scales always balance."

I would have pulled away, but Grandpa's gaze held a clarity I hadn't seen in years. He licked his lips, and his grip on my wrist tightened. "Her name was Katya. She lived down the road from me. She was beautiful—pale skin, long black hair, lips the colour of mulberries." His breath hitched and his eyes dropped to his lap. "Even when they found her broken, battered body in the stream behind our village, she was still beautiful."

"Everyone knew her husband did it, even if the *politsiya* could never prove it. He never moved. He just stayed in their house.

Within a year there was another beautiful young woman living there with him. The *babushkas* in the neighbourhood shook their heads, but what could be done? This was during one of the harshest winters we had seen in a decade. Food was scarce for everybody.

"One day I was out hunting in the woods by the lake. If I could take down a rabbit with my slingshot, we would have meat in the stew that night. It had gotten dark, but I was too hungry to give in just yet. The first sickle moon of spring was in the sky, giving me just enough light to see by. It was so cold. When I first saw the white shapes moving in the distance, I thought I was hallucinating. As I got closer I could see the shapes were women. They danced on the bank of the lake, barefoot in the grass. One of them had long black hair and lips the colour of mulberries. It was Katya."

"Then what? Grandpa? What happened next?"

But the moment had passed. His eyes stared into the distance, at something no one else could see. Pushing him now would only upset him.

Before the disease, my grandfather had been full of life, always willing to lend a hand or an ear. He could fix just about anything with his pocketknife and his wits alone. Now he was someone else—a stranger that lived in our home. He had helped to raise me. Now it was my turn to look after him. Both of my parents worked full-time, and we couldn't afford care, so I was the only option.

It was time for lunch. Ham and cheese sandwiches were the extent of my culinary skills, so that's what I made. As I pulled the ingredients from the fridge, my grandfather wandered into the kitchen and searched through cupboard doors.

Unable to find what he was looking for, he moved on to the drawers, pulling out utensils in order to search further into the depths.

When I turned to see what he was doing, the countertop was strewn with scissors, tongs, and the kitchen scales. "The scales always balance, hey Grandpa?" I'd meant it as a joke. Or at least I thought I did.

His eyes cleared and he looked right at me. "The Unquiet Dead. That's what they were. You would say 'siren' or 'spirit'. In Russian, *'rusalka'* or *'rusalki'*, for there were five. Women who had died violent deaths. Women who could not move on. Women who hungered for revenge. They haunt the waterways, leaving only to dance under the sickle moon. They delight in drowning men and forcing them to dance until they die. I had thought them only stories, but there was Katya.

"As if the mere thought of her name summoned her, she turned and saw me standing there. Her eyes were all black, like midnight on a starless night. I couldn't move. They came for me, taking my hands and leading me forwards. We began to dance."

He stopped, when he noticed the sandwich sitting in front of him. He started to eat, and I sighed. I had hoped he would hang on a little longer.

"Let an old man finish his lunch," he said.

Satisfied that the Alzheimer's hadn't crept back in, I poured him a glass of milk, pulled up a chair and waited.

When my grandfather finished eating he sat back and, with a contented sigh, continued. "I had never killed a man before, but when I hit Katya's husband with that rock I thought for sure he was dead."

"Wait, you missed a bit!" I interrupted.

"Did I?"

"Yes! The *rusalki* had caught you and forced you to dance."

"*Da.* Just making sure you were paying attention. Now, where was I?"

"We danced until my feet bled. Then we danced some more. I knew I was doomed. My heart raced. It was hard to catch my breath. When I stumbled, they laughed. When I tripped, they pulled me upright. I'm not too proud to tell you that I begged. I pleaded for my life. I said I would do anything, anything, if they would let me go. As one, they stopped. Anything? Katya said. Her voice was like dead leaves on the wind. What else could I say? I was not ready to die. So they told me what I could do to live. The *rusalki* whispered it into my ear and I . . ."

His eyes glazed over and he was gone again. The story couldn't be real, yet I was disappointed nonetheless. This was something different to the usual stories Grandpa told when he spoke about the old days. I had heard about his days of hockey glory and the time he ran across thin ice so many times I could recite them myself. But stories of homicidal ghosts? This was new.

I cleaned up the dishes as Grandpa wandered into the living room and turned the TV on. It wouldn't be long now before he fell asleep on the couch. Once I had finished tidying up, I dropped onto the couch beside him. He still had that vacant look in his eyes.

"You never killed a man before," I began, "but when you hit Katya's husband with that rock, you thought for sure he was dead."

Grandpa's chest heaved and he blinked several times.

I took his gnarled hand in mine, squeezing tight enough to feel the calluses on his palm.

He squeezed back, weaker than I expected, and continued his story. "I looked down at his limp body and saw his chest rise. I wasn't a murderer after all. At least, not yet. I picked up Katya's *muzh* and threw him over my shoulder. He was heavy, but I had been cutting and hauling timber all winter. I was used to carrying heavy loads. It was dark and late. There was no one to see me carry him into the woods.

"Katya's *muzh* groaned as I walked. He did not wake. It felt like an eternity before I reached the lake, an eternity in which to contemplate my actions. I was trading this man's life for my own. Surely he deserved it after what he had done? And what did I deserve?

"I laid his body down on the lake shore. The *rusalki* appeared like dreams from beneath the water, with only their hair to cover them. They gathered on the shore around the man. Katya knelt by his side and laid her cold, pale hand on his cheek.

His eyes fluttered before focusing on her. "Katya? It's you! You're alive?" he said.

She smiled, peaceful and benevolent. Without a word, she extended her hand and he took it. She drew him to his feet and it was only then that he began to realise. He took in his dead wife and her naked friends and the panic blossomed on his face. Too late, it was too late. They had him now.

"The *rusalki* wrapped their pale arms around him and dragged him into the lake. He struggled, but their grip was iron. Inexorably he was pulled into the water, deeper and deeper until his head disappeared under the surface. There was a mass of bubbles and he was gone.

"That was the first. It was awful. Yet it wasn't as hard as I thought it would be. I was used to survival. This was just another thing I had to do to live. The scales had to balance. The next for revenge were the twins . . ."

The ring of the phone startled me. I jumped up and caught it on the fourth ring. It was my mother checking in that everything was well. After assuring her that we were fine, I hung up the phone and hurried back to the living room, hoping my grandfather was still cognisant enough to continue his story. He was asleep on the couch, mouth open and snoring softly.

Trying not to be disappointed, I grabbed the remote and started flipping through the channels.

"I was watching that," a grumpy voice said. Grandpa was awake.

"Where was I up to?"

Nervous anticipation fluttered in my stomach. "You were up to the twins."

"*Da!* The twins. Mila and Lena were only sixteen when their father drowned them, one by one, in their own bathtub. When their mother found their lifeless bodies, water still dripping from their long red hair, she lost her mind. Their father blamed their mother for their deaths and she was committed to an asylum. Those girls were so mad. Even dead, their anger was a palpable force that surrounded them.

"By the time I stumbled into Mila and Lena, their father was an old man. In the end I just walked into the hospice and took him. Nobody cared. There was nobody left to love him. He struggled, of course. He knew his time on the scales was coming. But he couldn't get out of his wheelchair, so his efforts were in vain.

"I wheeled him right to the water's edge. The *rusalki* appeared, Mila and Lena leading them. They pulled him from his chair, his useless legs dragging behind him. He wept, though he no longer struggled. They played with him, the twins. Holding him under the water, then allowing him to surface for a quick breath of air before pulling him under again. I made myself watch. It was the hardest thing I had done so far in my life, watching that man suffer. But I did it. I was killing him as much as the *rusalki*." He stopped, his breath catching in his throat. His shoulders had slumped and he seemed smaller somehow.

"Why are you telling me this?" I asked.

"Because the scales always balance. Somebody should know," he said.

His answer confused me even more.

He reached over and took my hand. It was something he had never done before. "This is not an easy story," he said. "I would understand if you didn't want to hear anymore."

I took a moment to consider this. My grandfather believed what he was telling me. Alzheimer's was a cruel condition, taking a person away, bit by bit. During some of his worst bouts, my grandfather had said some very strange things. But this story was coherent, even if it wasn't believable. I owed it to him to hear it. And I wanted him to stay himself for as long as possible.

I gave his hand a squeeze. "Tell me the rest."

"Natalia's story was the worst. Her brother was not quite right. He pulled the wings off flies and threw bottle rockets at neighbourhood dogs. Her family's cat went missing and its collar was found in his room. One day when their parents were out, he cornered Natalia and tried to have his way with her. When she fought back, he beat her. He choked her to the point of unconsciousness, then let her breathe, over and over. He broke her legs. He broke her arms. He pulled her nails out. When he tired of playing with her, he took her to the bridge and threw her body into the river. She was still alive when she went into the water. That bastard stayed to watch her drown.

"Her parents thought she ran away, and her body was never found. Natalia's brother grew into a powerful man, both of body and *vliyaniye*. How do you say in English? Influence?"

I nodded, so he continued.

"He ran a gang of thugs who sold guns, drugs and murder for the right price. He was a professional criminal and I was a poor wood cutter. Getting to him would not be easy.

"I took a loan with one of his goons. I told him we had no money for food or clothes and that we may soon starve. It was even the truth. He gave me money and a high interest rate and three weeks to pay it back. Three weeks and one day later, Natalia's brother and his bandits came to visit. He liked to participate in the punishments he ordered."

A shudder ran through him. I had never seen my grandfather flinch at anything in my entire life. This man must have been awful.

"My family wasn't home that night, I had made sure of it. We could not afford electricity, only candles, so the house was dark when they arrived. Natalia's brother had brought two of his men with him and it didn't take them long to break in. He went in first, eager to begin.

"When only one of the bandits remained outside, I emerged from my hiding place and hit him in the head with the back of my axe. The sound of his body hitting the ground made the man in the doorway turn. I swung my axe, and he grabbed it. I let go, grabbed his head and drove it into the wall. I watched him fall, not seeing the fist coming for me. It hit so hard I almost blacked out. I dove forward, catching Natalia's brother around the waist. We grappled on the living room floor. He was bigger and stronger than I, he should have won. However, he wasn't used to victims who fought back. He began to tire, just enough that I got an arm around his throat. I held on as he struggled and fought. Eventually he went limp.

"I took no risks, tying his hands and feet. The other men I left where they had fallen. I loaded Natalia's brother into my wheelbarrow and headed for the lake.

"He woke up before I got there, tipping the wheelbarrow and fighting as best he could. I ended up dragging him the rest of the way. Natalia was waiting for us on the lake shore. She tore her brother from my hands, dragging him as if he weighed nothing. She dropped him in front of her sisters, who gathered around to pinch and scratch and bite. At first he didn't scream, remaining stoic in the face of their torment. It wasn't until they started to bite his fingers off, joint by joint, that he broke.

"He screamed through the loss of his fingers, his toes, his ears, his lips and his nose. When they took his manhood, he lost consciousness.

"He woke up when the cold water of the lake washed over his skin. They dragged him out deep and watched as he struggled. He tried to swim. He tried to scream. They watched as his mouth filled with water and he slid beneath the water. The *rusalki* followed his body down, Natalia stopping to blow me a kiss before she disappeared under the water. I threw up, then started the hike back home.

Grandpa went quiet for a long time after that. He looked pale and drawn after sharing such a difficult part of his story, and I couldn't help but notice the tremor in his hands.

I didn't want to push him, but my curiosity was stronger than ever. "What happened to the thugs left at your house?" I asked.

My grandfather sighed and rubbed his eyes. "They were gone when I returned. I took the money I had borrowed and brought my family here, where they would not be able to reach us. I am not proud of what I did to get us here, but I do not regret it."

"Wait. What about the fifth *rusalka*?" I said.

Another sigh, this time the exhalation made him shrink in on himself. "Vanya fell in love with a man who did not love her back. When she discovered his heart belonged to another, she cut her wrists in the bathtub and bled to death. I could not help her." A tear ran down his wrinkled cheek. "I need to rest." He held his hand out for me to help him up.

I pulled him from the couch and walked him to his room. He settled onto his bed and turned away from me.

I let him be and went back to the lounge room. I flicked through the channels, unable to settle on a program. My grandfather's tale had left me feeling melancholy and strange.

How did he come up with such a peculiar tale? Maybe it was a fairy tale he heard in his childhood? It seemed very graphic to be just a delusion brought on by the Alzheimer's. And why would my grandfather imagine himself a murderer? It felt like there was more to this story than there seemed. I was also haunted by the plight of the last *rusalka*. How could she ever get her revenge and find peace if she took her own life? Would her sisters wait for her or leave her behind all alone? I knew it wasn't real, it couldn't be. Still, I couldn't shake this lingering sense of doubt. It lasted all night, from the time my parents arrived home, through dinner, which Grandpa didn't join us for, until I went to bed. Thoughts chased themselves around my head, questioning everything I thought I knew about my grandfather. Even in sleep I felt restless. Voices filled my dreams, strident and upset. I woke to my mother shaking me. Her face was streaked with tears.

"Your grandfather is missing."

"Of course," I muttered, then couldn't figure out why I had said that. My mother hadn't heard, she was already gone.

My father was talking on the phone to the police. I dragged myself out of bed and went into my grandfather's room. His sheets were rumpled and his bathrobe was gone. There was a photo propped on his bedside table that I had never seen before. It was of a beautiful woman with blonde hair and blue eyes. I picked the photo up and turned it over. 'Vanya' was written on the back.

It all made sense now.

"I know where he is!" I yelled, running out of his room and down the stairs.

"Where?" my mother cried from the kitchen.

I didn't stop. It was already too late, but I had to try.

Once out the back door, I took off at a sprint across the yard. There was a path through the trees that led to a park. A small river bordered the far side of the park. I ran all the way to its bank, stopping dead when I saw what I had feared—my grandfather's robe and slippers in a neat pile on the riverbank.

I stared at the river. There was no sign of him. He was already gone.

My mother arrived behind me and fell to her knees.

"The scales always balance," I murmured as she began to wail.

About the Author:

LJ McLeod lives in Queensland, Australia. She works in Pathology and writes in her spare time. She has been published in several anthologies and has been nominated twice for the Aurealis Award. In her spare time she enjoys diving, reading and travelling.

When Themis Does Not Return

Munira Tabassum Ahmed

They say there is no wrath is this glorious justice.

The asphalt is warmer than I remember;
concrete body heats up quicker in this
near-summer ache. We melt into the
metal cool of a megacorp's supermarket
and sway in this clinical blue-white.
Rest there. They say there is no harm.
The speakers hum to life. Ever-repeating.
"Fear not our knife-sharp teeth, but the
decaying flowers in your own men."
Ever-repeating. Ever-repeating. Ever-repeating.

Tomorrow morning we will wake and breathe in the
same air as yesterday; only thicker, only more bitter.
For now, we reimagine our past.

There is no word for justice anymore.

We balance on the sword Themis
left behind, not knowing which side is fact or
fiction, not knowing whether *we* are fact or fiction.
If we fall to one side, we may cease to exist
and that is the price we pay in this heat.

They're finalising the purchase of this country tomorrow.
The land will swelter sweet under new leadership;
countrymen holding up a nation that no longer belongs
to them. We look down at our teeth, only
to see them blunted. There is no revolution left.
Our limbs remain crushed like the fruit of a
lilly pilly tree under the heel of a once-holy man.

Tonight we mourn our future,
no more time to reimagine our past.

There is no justice in this glorious wrath.

About the Author:

Munira Tabassum Ahmed is a young Bangladeshi-Australian poet and performer. As a performance poet, she has placed third in the NSW Finals of the Australian Poetry Slam (2019) and has featured at Bankstown Poetry Slam and Westside Poetry Slam. She won the inaugural Australia ReMade poetry competition and her work has been published in Voiceworks, The Lifted Brow, the United Nations' Global Advocate, the Sonora Review, Aniko Press and elsewhere.

THE SECRETS SHE EATS

Nikky Lee

Not all secrets are given willingly. Sometimes I have to hunt them from street to street, town to town. They run, scramble, try to weasel their way out of my grip, slippery things that they are. Often they beg, sometimes they cry. And sometimes, once they're cornered and at a dead end, they simply stand there, resigned and waiting for my final reckoning.

I blow into town like a tumbleweed on the wind. A woman in black, cloaked and hooded. Knife in my belt, pistol on my hip and boots crusted with mud. The villagers don't see my face, not straight away, but they are not fooled.

"Eater." The whisper announces my arrival, rushing ahead of me in undertones. Along the dusty main street it goes, passing through blacksmith and tailor's shops, into the saloon. In an hour it will have reached the plains; a day later, the plateau beyond.

They know what I am. And yet, there's something in my step that makes them turn; in the 'swish-click' of my boots that mesmerises. Something in my scent that draws the villagers in, like moths to a flame.

The first one staggers out of the saloon and finds me there in the street. There's distilled spirits on his breath and a pink flush on his dusty cheeks. He's young, pretty-like; soft brown curls grace his brow.

"I love Josie Fisher," he tells me.

The words roll over me like a sprinkling of sweet breadcrumbs. I lick them up, savouring each one. Barely a snack, but I'll take it. I nod and he turns away, his shoulders relaxing, an ecstasy of relief on his face.

"I love Josie Fisher," he says again, walking away in a daze.

An innocent secret. A smile twitches my lips. They're not particularly filling, but they are sweet. A footstep crunches at my back and I turn. An older woman is there, a hessian bag of groceries abandoned in the dirt. She trembles as she approaches. Her blue eyes dart to my hood, then away again, even as her mouth opens, revealing yellowed teeth. "I stole my husband's best horse to buy milk of the poppy," she murmurs.

Ah, a secret with a little more meat. The weight of it eases into my belly, a tasty morsel. But there's more, I can smell it as sure as I smell the horse shit swept into the gutters. I peel back my hood and the woman's eyes lock with mine. She quivers like a marmot caught in the glare of a snake.

"And?" I prompt.

She hugs her arms about herself. "I told him vagabonds did it. He went out searching for them and came back with fever. It's bad this year, you know? Real bad. Young Sally it took. And the Miller's wife."

Her words are like tiny steaks on my tongue. Juicy. Succulent. I breathe them in, relishing their taste. I nod again and a gasp whistles out of her. She sinks to her knees and releases a sob: her burden suddenly dissolved. I step away and she frowns as she finds herself slumped in the middle of the street. She picks herself up. With deft strokes, she beats the dust out of her skirts, picks up her shopping and walks off.

Perhaps now she'll have the courage to make it right. If not, well, I'll get another meal later.

I set up shop in the saloon. Soon they come, sweet and tender alike. They can't help themselves. A line forms out the door. Clearly it's been many a year since one of us has come through these parts. One by one, they sit down at my table and lean in to whisper their guilt.

"I stole a drunkard's shoes last winter." This from a girl in a woollen sweater patched over and over at the elbows.

"I put salt on Mary Cole's cake at the last town cake competition," a busty woman admits, wringing her gloves.

A sheepish grin from a grey-haired man. "I have a mistress. Every Thursday." That one barely touches the sides as it goes down. He'll come back later for sure.

"I wagered my father's fortune in cards and lost." From a gaunt young man in a fine cloak and polished shoes.

"I hate my children."

"When customers piss me off, I spit in their soup."

"I fucked a cow once." That one made me blink twice.

On and on. Bit by bit, their secrets fill me. Albeit briefly. When the afternoon shadows lengthen, Vander the barkeep lights the hearth and a slow heat creeps into the emptying saloon. The line waiting on me thins and clears with the coming of night. Fear of the dark overrides their instinct to spill their burdens. I curse under my breath. My mouth craves that big something I'd followed into town. Big and thick and heavy. Like wild bison roasting on a spit. It's here somewhere. I know it. Something I could sink my teeth into one hundred times over.

A throat clears next to me. My gaze swings back to the thin, dark haired man—a boy really—sat in the opposite chair, waiting. I'd scarcely noticed him.

"Yes, yes," I say absently, and reach for my drink. Alcohol doesn't sate me the way a good secret might, but it dampens the craving. Then I get a whiff of him; of his secret. I freeze, scenting the air between us. Not quite the same *big* I'd been hunting, but there's a kinship there. Something . . . important.

The boy shifts uncomfortably in the seat, straightens his too-big, probably hand-me-down, vest. His nails are bitten to the quick.

"I'm listening," I say.

"I, um . . ." His fingers twist and writhe, nimble-like, a tailor's apprentice perhaps or a jeweller's. They clench together as he clears his throat. "I saw something the other night." A gulp. "Something strange."

The magic rises in my belly, but I hold it at bay. The boy is twitchy, like a rabbit ready to duck back into his burrow if I push him too hard. This is a secret that needs teasing out. I sip my drink, trying not to let my interest show too much. "Go on."

"I was coming home late two nights ago," the boy begins. "Closed up shop like Mr. Cole asked and cut across Roper's field. I know I shouldn't but it was late, you know, and Da was waiting at home; he gets anxious when I'm out past tea. Roper's field is just grazing for his horses, and they're all trained gentle-like, wouldn't kick a gnat if it landed on them wrong, so I figured no harm done. I've taken that way plenty of times before."

He pauses as Vander arrives and places an ale on the table before him—and lingers. "Any dinner, ma'am?"

"No, thank you."

Vander is still for a long moment, before slowly turning for the kitchens. I sigh. I knew his type; clever like a vulture and ready to wring every coin he can.

The boy furrows his brow at the drink, then reaches for his pocket.

"It's on me," I say and wave my hand. "Continue."

"Well, two nights ago, I took the short cut, like always. But halfway through I heard a grinding sound," his lips purse, evidently trying to think of a way to describe it. "A pestle on mortar sound. Then cracking a few steps later, like sticks breaking. I froze, thinking it was perhaps a horse having a roll in the grass, or rubbing his back on a fence post, but then I saw sparks from a flint . . ." He shifts back in his seat as I lean in. Then realises what he's done and flushes.

"And?" I ask, unperturbed.

"I rushed at it. Think I even shouted, 'Hey, what're you doing?' Or maybe I thought it. Either way, lighting a fire in a grass field was asking for it to go up like a tinderbox. I wasn't raised a farmer, but even I know that." His eyes go distant, and he shivers, then takes a pull of his ale. "What I found, well; it was a fire, trapped in a stone circle, but the . . . *thing* next to it. I don't know what it was. But it wasn't human—I'm sure of that."

"What did it look like?"

The boy stares into his mug. "Ugly. Wrinkles all about the face." He traces a finger along his cheeks and jowls. "Snout for a nose. And small, squat. Like someone sat on it."

"And what did it say?" I ask.

The boy is silent for a long moment. "Nothing," he says at last into his ale. A deeper flush creeps up his throat and into his ears. "I screamed and ran away."

I nod, running a light finger over my empty glass. "Wise move," I muse, wishing he'd paid more attention to its appearance; I can name a hundred fey clans the creature might belong to. But a lead is a lead, and I yearn for something juicy. I stand. "Show me."

Aben, for I've learned that is his name, rests a hand on the fence paling. "In there," he says, pointing into the dark field. And it is truly dark, no kerosene lamps this part of town and there's little light beyond what our lantern provides—even to my eyes. Not that my eyes are much to brag about. I'm not fae-sighted like my father. I have my mother's eyes. Mortal eyes.

And a fae's hunger.

I set the oil lamp down on the post and listen. Grass stalks chitter in the breeze. The fence creaks ever so slight. I frown.

"What is it?" Aben asks.

"No insects."

"Tucked in for the night?" he suggests, the edge of a coy smile quirking his mouth. When I don't respond, he coughs and looks down at his shoes. They're well made, shiny iron buckles polished to a gleam. A shoemaker's apprentice then.

I sigh, set a foot on the bottom rung of the fence and swing a leg over.

Aben swings his leg over too.

"What are you doing?"

He stares at me dumbly, as if the answer is obvious. "Coming with you of course."

I snort. "No, you're not."

His eyebrows bunch. "I can't let a lady go out there on her own."

"Do I look like I need your protection?" I raise an eyebrow in return.

He considers me a moment there, straddled on the fence, gaze travelling to my calloused hands, the knife on my hip and the pistol holstered under my cloak. "No," he admits and shrinks into himself, looking more boyish than ever. "But I want to show people I'm not a coward. I can do more than run away."

The words hit me like a sucker punch. A memory rises up: my mother dabbing a rag on my torn lip and me, ten years old, saying *"I'm not a monster. I want to show them."*

"You will," my mother says in the same, tired tone of a parent listening to a conversation so old it's worn holes in its sleeves. *"Give them time."*

My fists clench. *"I want to show them now!"*

And mother's patient words, *"Give them time."*

Atop the fence, I roll my eyes. "Stay behind me."

Aben beams and scrambles over the pilings.

We creep through the field, lantern held high, dry grass scratching our legs. Halfway in, we stumble into a clearing where the grass is flattened—not trampled but carefully squashed down so that in another day or two it might spring back. A small stone circle lies in the middle, ashes cold.

"This was it," Aben says, there's an edge to his voice as he turns in a circle and squints into the dark. He stands so close his back brushes mine. The lantern in his hand quivers and the sphere of light around us wobbles.

"Relax," I tell him. Taking the lantern, I bend down to examine the ashes. "There's nothing here." I crunch a piece of charcoal in my hand and sniff. And there, underneath the smoke and soot birch, lavender and rosemary.

"Were you always a secret eater?" Aben asks from over my shoulder. His voice is stronger now, more confident.

"Always."

Aben's forehead rumples into a frown. "And you've been doing this all your life? Journeying from town to town, relieving people of their secrets." He pauses. "Why don't I feel your power pulling at me anymore?"

"What's to say you're not?" I dust my hands off, catch a glimpse of his face and laugh. As a rule, I don't pray on people's insecurities once they fess whatever is on their mind—that's a sure way to get run out of town, but his shock catches me off guard. "It doesn't work like that."

"It doesn't?"

"I can't force you to tell your secrets. Deep down you've got to be willing. If you have a secret you'd never tell anyone, I can't force it out of you." Those are the ones I hunt, when they have the right scent; rich and with full copper notes. I make a show of leaning close to him and taking a whiff. "You don't have the smell, you're all leather and pomegranates since I took your secret. At most, you'll have a slight inclination to tell the truth for a few days"—I cock a grin at him—"depending how headstrong you are. I've had married men fess their adultery then walk straight back into a brothel."

Aben doesn't answer, but his eyes follow me as I pick my way across the clearing, pausing at two rocks nestled in the flattened grass. Both are smooth, one wide and flat, the other round and about the same size as my head. Residue cakes one side of each. I run a finger down the head-sized rock, hold it to my nose. Lavender and rosemary. "You were right about the mortar and pestle," I say, wiping my hand on my cloak.

My companion squeaks a response. Actually squeaks, like his voice has been caught on a hook and yanked out of water. I turn to find him standing rigid, the tip of a rusted knife jutting up at his throat. At the other end of the knife is a squat figure wearing old children's clothes, patched and threadbare.

"What you want?" the creature hisses through a frog-like mouth and its perfectly round eyes narrow into slits. Hair hangs limp and straggled from its brow, like it has been out in the weather too long. Behind it, a mound of sticks and firewood lay scattered on the grass.

I hold my hands out for peace. "Easy, we mean no harm. What's your name, friend?"

"Dalziel."

"And what are you, a boggart?"

"Broonie," the fae spits. "No boggart here."

My gaze wanders those ragged clothes again, then to the rows of scars on the back of his exposed forearms. Layers upon layers of them, turning his skin to knots of puckered scar tissue. He might have been a broonie once, but not anymore. Bad luck or perhaps a bad contract has transformed him from household hearth spirit to homeless sprite. Either way, he's old fae, from across the sea. My nose twitches, catching a lingering whiff of a copper secret. As if he senses it too, Dalziel's knife presses under Aben's jaw, all he has to do is stab up.

"What are you?" Dalziel snarls. "You look human, but you don't smell like one."

I open my palms to him and slowly crouch so we're closer to eye level. "I am a secret eater."

"Pah, lies. Eaters aren't real. Just stories."

"I assure you we're not. Not on this continent, anyway."

"Eater," Aben's voice squeezes out. He makes eyes at me, casting a meaningful look at my pistol.

Dalziel's grip tightens on his knife.

"It's fine," I assure them both. "Aben, broonies like Dalziel are harmless fae. A few pranks, nothing sinister. Dalziel, Aben is a harmless human, he wants to be friends."

Dalziel's knife eases off Aben's jawline, but still hovers close to Aben's throat.

"He'll trade you his shoes, in a show of good faith," I add.

Dalziel's eyes light up. "Oh, why didn't you say sooner?" It's impossible to miss the excitement in Dalziel's voice. He kicks off his worn boots, all cracked leather and flapping soles, and holds them out to Aben.

Aben shoots me a glare. "I will not—"

I cut him off with a glare of my own, until he sighs and reaches for his polished shoes.

"No buckles," Dalziel says.

Aben frowns a beat, then, "Oh right, iron." Even out here, everyone knows fae can't abide it. He loosens the buckles off, puts them in his pocket, and reluctantly holds his shoes out.

The knife drops away, sheathing back into Dalziel's belt. "My thanks, friend Aben." The boggart drops to his bottom and pulls Aben's shoes on with obvious glee. His feet, I notice, are scarred too—thin white strikes across each arch. The shoes are too big, but Dalziel's up and strutting around in them like Aben has handed him gold clogs. Then he turns on Aben, blinking his round eyes expectantly.

"Put on his shoes," I whisper to Aben, motioning to the discarded items on the grass. "It'll seal your concord."

Aben's face twitches like he wants to object, but under Dalziel's watch he bends down and slides his feet into the old shoes. His toes poke through the holes at the tip like they're a pair of sandals.

"Wonderful! Our friendship is set." Dalziel claps his hands and admires his new feet again. "Very nice gift," he says. "A nice gift indeed. Our friendship will be grand!"

"How long do I have to wear these?" Aben murmurs to me.

"Until we leave his domain." I gesture to the field.

Aben sighs, resigned to his fate. "What about you? Don't you need to trade?"

"I'm getting to it." I raise my voice, catching Dalziel by the shoulder as he hops about. Again, that copper whiff. Very faint. But it's there. I focus my attention on him. It's harder to work my power on fae, but I can if the secret is strong enough. And with the right kind of probing. "Friend Dalziel, why are you out in this field burning lavender and rosemary?"

Dalziel's eyes turn glassy, his face relaxes. Tranced. I grimace: I've pushed too hard. I ease off, releasing my hand from his grubby coat and coaxing him to sit at the edge of the pit. Dalziel blinks, shakes himself and starts building a fire, a house for the flame from his sticks and wood.

"What's with the lavender and rosemary?" I ask again, motioning to the two stones and the fresh bundles of herbs waiting to be pulped.

"To ease the bones," Dalziel says simply, as if the answer is obvious.

Aben and I share a confused look. "Your bones?"

Dalziel snorts. "Dead bones." He thumps his chest. "Not these. These still have plenty of life left in them. The bones under here." He stomps one foot, indicating the earth below.

Copper fills my nostrils. I'm getting close. I lean in, eager. "There are bodies buried here?"

Aben's face drains of colour. "Bodies?" he squeaks and he crosses himself. Funny how humans get all squeamish about these things.

Dalziel busies himself with the fire, lighting it with a practised strike from a knife and flint. He's been out here a while it seems.

"How many bodies?" I ask.

Dalziel considers. "Many. Dozens. Maybe more."

Another wick up my nose. My magic prowls in, hungry. *Closer, closer.* I press him a tiny bit more. "Who puts them there?"

Dalziel stiffens, back turning rigid, his hands clamp tight around his flint stone. *He knows.* Gods and spirits sure. He knows. Dalziel's eyes find mine, bathwater grey and glistening in the firelight. "Don't make me say," he begs. The hand around the flint quivers, and what I'd mistook for tense caution reveals itself: blind fear. It's so strong I could poke out my tongue and lick it off the air.

"Please," I say. "It's important." I gesture to the field. "And don't they deserve justice?"

Dalziel stares after my finger, eyes glazing over.

Damn, I've pressed too close again. For a fae as susceptible as this, he must have human ancestry in him, like me. Maybe not half-half like me, but it's there. Inside my chest, something I thought tough and hardened squeezes. It's not easy straddling two worlds. You never fully step into one or the other, it's always a balancing act between the two.

"My apologies," I say and shuffle back, my stomach giving a disappointed gurgle.

Dalziel opens his mouth, tries to speak, fails, then works his lips as if trying to chew through a particularly tough bit of bread.

Aben eases down on Dalziel's other side. His face is still pale, but his gaze is tender. He pats the boggart's back. "We're here," he assures. "One word at a time."

"I . . . c-can't!" Dalziel manages, spittle flying, straining to get the words out. It takes all his willpower.

Understanding clicks. I curse under my breath. "He's been Compulsed."

Aben lifts his head, concern rippling across his brow. "He's been what?"

"Compulsed. A spell. Stops him talking to anyone about this. Nasty stuff." Before I can think, I am up and pacing. Nervous habit. I swear again and cast my sights nightward. I would have been perfectly happy with a simple serial killer, but no. "We're dealing with wicked magic." I glance at Dalziel. "Nod if I'm right."

He nods.

"Shit."

There goes my easy meal.

"Anyone can use wicked magic," I explain to Aben. "You just need the knowledge." *And a spell book.* But the less people who know that the better.

Around us, leathers and needlework of his shoemaker's shop line the walls. It was the easiest place for us to confer out the way of prying eyes. Next to Aben, Dalziel looks miserable. The lamplight shows his limp grey hair, owl eyes dim and cheeks sallow from exhaustion. That's what a secret like this does to a person—fae or man. In this we're all the same.

Aben grips Dalziel's forearm and gives it a reassuring shake. "We'll find a way to remove the Compulsion, I promise."

A tick of annoyance twitches in my jaw. He is right. I'll grant him that. No one deserves to live with a copper secret eating them up from the inside. But Aben makes his promise with the conviction of one who has never dealt with wicked magic before.

Dalziel swallows and nods. "My thanks, friend Aben."

We sink into a stony silence. "So many people," Aben murmurs. We'd questioned Dalziel best we could on the way to the shop, keeping to the backstreets. The total count before Dalziel managed a nod: thirteen.

And those are the ones he knows about, I think but don't say.

Aben rubs his eyes. "How did no one notice?"

To this, at least, I have an answer. "Easy. Disguise their deaths as something else. Who in town has died recently? And what did they die of?"

Aben falls still, his fingers pinching his chin as he considers. "Sally Barton, fever. Bobby Ruthford"—his eyes dart up to mine—"fever. Frederick Sawyers." He swallows. "Fever. Those were all in the last month."

My gut knots. "All unrelated? No contact? They weren't family or neighbours? Or lovers?"

Aben shakes his head. "Not that I know."

I curse. "Then it's not a normal fever."

"But I *went* to Bobby's funeral, he was buried in the church cemetery," Aben objects.

My eyebrow cocks. "And did you see the body?"

Aben pauses, then shakes his head, uncertainty dawning on his face. "It was a closed casket."

An empty casket more like. No need to say it, it's clear from the horror on Aben's face that it's occurred to him too.

"But why bury them in the field?" Aben asks.

"Hiding—" Dalziel manages before the compulsion cuts his words short and reduces him to a coughing fit.

"It's all right Dalziel, I know," I assure him, patting the boggart's arm. With a glance to Aben, I add, "They're snatching the bodies before anyone gets too good a look and hiding them in Roper's field." My mind darts back to the woman who'd given up her secret on the town road; who'd sold her husband's horse to buy milk of the poppy. What had she said? *He went out searching for his horse and came back with fever.*

Where, then, had he gone? And what had he seen that he shouldn't have? I come to my feet. "The woman with the poppy addiction, where does she live? I need to talk to her husband."

Aben scowls, his hands clenching into fists on the table. "There's more than one woman with poppy addiction here. In case you hadn't noticed." Curious. A sore point I hadn't expected.

I raise an eyebrow at him and he sighs.

"My brother got mixed up in the trade. Didn't end well. Swore I'd stay the hell away from it."

Dalziel places a hand on Aben's forearm and pats it gently. "Please friend, this is important," the broonie croaks out, skirting around the edge of his secret. I suck in a breath, scenting the air on my tongue. I'm on to something. When Dalziel glances up at me and gives the faintest of nods, I know I'm right.

Aben sees it too. He closes his eyes, takes a moment, then releases his fists. "Describe her."

I do, and his brow wrinkles. "Sounds like Macey Gruber."

"And her husband is ill?"

Aben nods.

"Take me there."

We find the grave in Macey Gruber's front garden. Its earth is freshly turned and stinks of copper, the scent lies on the mound thick as a snowdrift. My hunger stirs with a faint gurgle. *Soon,* I promise it. From inside the farmer's cottage, a woman wails.

"We're too late," Aben says.

"Not necessarily."

When we knock, a bloodshot, tear-streaked face greets us. She's barely coherent enough to talk, but she opens the door and starts making tea. I sigh and take the teapot away and sit her down at the table. Her clothes are dirty, gravel soil still stuck to them. Five miles from town and on her own, she'd had to do the deed herself. My heart twists, thinking of another grave far from here and the mother I'd buried in it. That hurt never truly leaves you. It fades into the background, scabs over and scars, but never goes away. Not completely.

"It's my fault," Macey Gruber says, staring at her hands. There's dirt under her ragged nails. She fidgets, anxious in her own skin.

I rest my hands on hers and flex my magic. "Where did he go when he went looking for his horse?"

Macey Gruber stills, her pupils dilating. I don't like using my power like this, smothering people with it. I can't force people to talk, but I can make their tongues loose; fill their heads with haze until the world turns so dream-like the secret just slips out.

Macey sways, her head rolls to one side. "All the way to the plateau." She closes her eyes and relaxes into my magic like it's a warm bath. "That feels nice."

"Up to the fae kingdom?" Aben whispers. "I knew it! They did something—ow!"

Dalziel stamps on his foot. "Fae don't work wicked magic!" Dalziel protests, and he wants to say more, but the Compulsion chokes the words in his throat. He works his jaw for a moment, a vein pops in his head, cheeks flushing with anger, then gives up with a "humph!"

"It's outlawed," I explain to Aben. "Work wicked magic and you're cast out. Magic sealed. No longer fae. Few dare risk it. Is that what we're looking for Dalziel? An outcast?"

Dalziel shakes his head.

"Human then." At this, a copper scent curls off my words, strong and delicious. I'm closing in. I take Macey's hands again, give her a little shake.

Her eyelids flutter open. "Let me sleep," she groans. "It's all my fault. Let me sleep forever."

"Why is it your fault, Macey?"

A long pause and her red eyes, too red to be just from crying, study my face. "I sold his horse. His favourite." The smell of the old secret fills my nose like stale bread. Dry and ordinary. I've not asked the right question. "Who did you sell it to?"

"Vander."

The name drops into my belly like a bite of marinated pork. Full bodied flavour rolls over my tongue. Copper fills my nose. I breathe it in, chest swelling, my mind revelling in it. It's *here*. The trail's *here*.

"Vander, the *barkeep*?" Aben interrupts, incredulous. "What would he want with a farm hor—" but I hold up a hand for quiet.

"Why Vander? Why did you go to him?"

Macey swallows, sensing she's on the edge of spilling it all. "Because he has the poppy," she whispers. "He runs it all."

Got you.

Copper hooks my nose, pulling my head around. A trail flares to life in my mind's eye, burning a path to my quarry like a line of gunpowder. It points straight back to town.

Dalziel grunts. Aben and I glance over to find him twitching on the floor, nodding furiously between his spasms. Once Dalziel sees we've noticed, he slumps, utterly spent. Aben hurries over, sits him up.

"Easy. Breathe," he says.

"Water," Dalziel croaks. "Please, friend Aben." Aben fetches a cup and the cold kettle from Macey's stove and Dalziel gulps it down.

"Stay here," I tell them, striding for the door. My trail beckons.

Aben's hand closes around my elbow. "I'm coming."

For a heartbeat I consider telling him no, that it's dangerous. Human my quarry might be, but he's got wicked magic at his disposal, and I can't protect Aben from it.

"Please."

His request turns to a bitter taste in my mouth. Not quite a secret—at least not the kind I like. It mingles with the copper, defiling it with its guilt. A secret blame then. That he'd turned his back when he should have helped. Of all times to grow a conscience. My gaze roves the room as I try to find the right words to explain why coming with me is a bad idea, the worst idea actually. My eyes light on the corner of a small envelope poking out of the pocket in Macey's dress. When I bend down to pull it loose, her hand catches my sleeve.

"Stay," she begs, rousing from her dream-state. In hindsight, working my magic on a poppy addict might not have been such a wise play. "Don't go." She claws at my clothes.

I detach her fingers one by one and slip the envelope into the fire at the hearth. It goes up in a heady whiff of burned poppy powder. "I have to," I tell her. The trail calls. But I don't like the idea of leaving her here alone. She needs more help than I can give.

Dalziel stands up with a grimace and dusts off his coat. "I will look after her," he says.

Aben cast me a doubtful look. "I thought you said he was a prankster."

"Broonies are not pranksters," Dalziel huffs. "We help." He pauses and the flicker of a grin crosses his wide mouth. "If the trade is right."

I study the squat fae. Maybe I read him wrong, perhaps there was more of the broonie left in him that I'd thought. After all, he'd been trying to appease the dead in Roper's field. If I gave him this chance, might he return to the fireside spirit he'd once been?

I crouch before him so we're eye level. "You would do this for me?"

Dalziel nodded, then held up one finger. "On one condition."

"Here we go," Aben muttered, attention dropping to his second-hand shoes. He'd not had a chance to change them.

"Name it."

Dalziel motioned me close, "Stop the bastard." His eyes snare me with their intensity and there's something pleading in them. Something he cannot say. "*Please.*"

"I suppose it makes sense," Aben says through a yawn as we watch the saloon from across the street, waiting for the last of its patrons to stagger out. Our alley stinks of horse shit, cat piss and garbage, but it's the best we've got. Now that I've found the trail, the scent of copper hangs over the place, thick as soup. Coats the saloon like sticky paint. In my pockets, my fingers itch something chronic, begging for release.

"All those shipments from the coast. I thought it was just ale," Aben says. He rubs his face and slaps his cheeks to keep himself awake. "He has them bring it right up Main Street, you know. I can't count the number of times I've seen a cart full of kegs and the like parked out front with men unloading it—all of it in broad daylight! I never thought to question. No one has."

"No one alive," I correct him. If I had to guess, more than one corpse in Roper's field was there simply because they'd gotten too curious. A bit of wicked magic and they fell sick and died. Then whisk the body away and bribe the undertaker to keep the funeral casket shut. Job done.

Only it wasn't that simple. Wicked magic *always* had a cost.

My hands curl into fists as I think of Dalziel. Compelled to aid a murderer and not tell a soul. I can imagine how it happened. A contract of servitude to a smuggler in exchange for conveyance across the sea. Ten years, maybe twenty; a small price for a long-lived fae. Worth the risk for new life on a new continent, far away from the feuding and bloodshed of the old world. Only, his contract had been sold on to the likes of Vander once the ship arrived at port. It's a sad and all too common story.

At last, the final patron sways out the double doors and the lamp-lit windows turn dark. I glance at the moon; three, perhaps four o'clock in the morning.

I flex my fingers, feeling the prick of claws under my nails. Time to move, before this secret has a chance to escape.

We slink out from the alleyway. The moon's out and high, casting long drifts of shadow across the street. Aben follows doggedly behind. I'd tried to talk him out of coming, but he wouldn't hear of it. And from the stubborn set of his jaw, I'd known better than to argue, else he follow and give the hunt away. No, best he see this through to its end where I can keep an eye on him. With any luck, I won't give him nightmares.

Across the street and into the saloon. Aben catches the double doors so they don't swing behind us.

And there he is.

Waiting. The cold barrel of a '76 Winchester pointed our way.

"You picked the wrong night to be nosey, Eater."

Like I said. Some secrets beg. Some cry. Some do nothing at all. And some, when cornered with no way to run, turn around and bite.

Vander levels the shotgun at us.

The world sinks into fragments of time. A slick, copper-laden breath filling my lungs. I dive for Aben; pushing him to the floor.

Vander's rifle cracks. One saloon door erupts into shards of wood.

The next beat I'm up and running, leaving Aben reeling on the floor.

Vander aims his gun again. Too slow. Much too slow for my fae blood all frenzied with the hunt.

I dodge, my vision turning to a blur of hunger and shadow. A bullet whisks past my shoulder, snags a hole in the wall.

Vander's growl fills my ears, anger turning desperate. I close in, ten paces between us. He cocks the rifle again, aims for my chest.

Before I can think, before reason or judgement sets in, my body twists.

Jumps.

The bullet finds my gut. Buries deep and gnaws with a gusto that brings me to my knees. I stagger, clutching my belly.

"Ha, got you, fairy bitch," Vander snarls. He glances up to the balustrade where a small squat figure is waiting. "Another one for the field, Freda." The figure's perfectly round eyes fix on the scene below, frog mouth pinched shut. Another broonie. This one is softer than Dalziel, younger too, her hair thick and swamp green. But there are features I recognise. Dalziel's ears. Dalziel's nose. His kin through and through.

No wonder he was so insistent I end this.

She doesn't move.

"Freda!" Vander barks.

The broonie juts her jaw, squares her shoulders and stays still. Below, blood oozes from between my fingers. I'm too far gone to feel pain, but soon the weakness will seep in. I lurch to my feet.

Vander curses, snatches a switch-knife from the bar and scores it down his forearm. He utters something unintelligible under his breath. The blood oozing from the gash evaporates, exposing the open rent of flesh. Pressure washes over the room. I feel it wrap around my limbs and squeeze me still, right down to my itching fingers. *Wicked magic.* Damn, I'd gotten sloppy. I search for Aben but can't find him. *Double damn.*

"Freda," Vander growls.

Above, the broonie's legs jerk, pulling her down the stairs.

"Why all this?" I ask. My seized jaw slurs the words together. It's not much of a question but it's all I can think of to buy time. Some secrets can't resist bragging when they're exposed. I hope Vander is one of them.

Vander pauses, a slight curl in his lip. "What does it matter?"

"Matters . . . to me," I say, forcing the words through my teeth. "To the people left . . . behind."

Vander shrugs and nonchalantly flicks his knife open and shut. Open and shut. "Truth be I've forgotten why."

His words slide down my throat and into my belly in juicy morsels. But I want more. "Why use sickness then?"

Vander pauses, considering me. "Some couldn't pay, some wouldn't, some threatened to expose my operations. Bad business leaving them to talk." He comes closer, flicks his switch-knife out again under my jaw. "You really should have bought dinner."

It comes together in a heartbeat.

"You feed them cursed food." I swallow and fight to raise my voice. "An easy thing, I imagine, to cut yourself and work a spell behind a kitchen door instead of behind a bar." I still can't see Aben, but I hope he's listening.

Vander studies me, curious, as if I'm a puzzle he hasn't figured out yet. "It is."

"Why not poison?" It would be easier. I eye the gash on his forearm. If it took that much blood to work a binding, how much more to work a spell of killing? I think of Dalziel's scars; those hundreds of white lines scoured into his skin and probably Freda's too. Rage boils inside me.

"Poison's too expensive. No money in it." Vander's tone is dry, matter of fact.

All about the money, eh? That's the thing with wicked magic, it can get you what you want, but it turns you cold inside. Once, he might have been an honest merchant, but the magic sunk in,

49

twisted it all up, turned his morals inside out. It's one cost few recognise until it's too late.

Vander's switchblade wanders along my chin and my jaw relaxes at its touch. I work my mouth open, testing this sliver of freedom he's granted. It's not much. He flicks his wrist, and the tip of his knife burns a line across my cheek.

"Ow!"

His eyes fixate on that first red line. Then the knife quivers close again, pauses above my other cheek, then shifts to my forehead, as if he's debating where to cut next. "To think of the spells I might cast with your fae blood," he whispers. And there's excitement there. A man enthralled in the power of magic. He presses closer and the scent of his sweat and blood fills my nose. Rich and coppery.

My mouth salivates. I bite down on my hunger. "You've fucked up."

He frowns, steps back, suddenly unsure. I suppose he's used to his victims begging—at least the victims he finished like this.

"You stopped counting us," I say, and grin.

Vander's eyes search me, then dart to Freda still standing at the bottom of the staircase. Realisation dawns on him in a slackening of his face, a strickening in his eyes. He whirls—just in time to see Aben plunge a meat cleaver into a leather-bound book.

Just like we planned.

It's no light cut, Aben throws his whole body behind the blow. The blade sinks through the cover as if it's made of butter, slices through the marrow of pages and thuds into the wood of the bar underneath. It sticks there like an axe in a tree stump.

His spell book is the source of his power. I'll distract him while you find it. That had been our agreement going in. I almost thought it hadn't worked.

"NO!" Vander's shriek turns my hairs on end. He lunges for Aben, even though it's too late. Far, far too late. His spell sloughs away, releasing my limbs.

Time to feed.

My fae blood boils. A burn building in my gut around Vander's gunshot. Copper swims up my nose, into my lungs, driving the hunger deeper. In a heartbeat, my *chelae* extend from my fingers, long flexible claws, strong as steel, sharp as swords. One set catches Vander in the boot, piercing through leather and sole to the floor beneath. He howls and buckles to cradle his trapped leg. My second set locks around his ribs in a cage, thumb and fingers pincering him still then drags him down in a sprawl.

I'm on him in a blur, straddling his chest. Pain flares in my belly. *Soon.* I tell it. *Just a little more.* Anticipation pulls my lips into a grin.

"Don't touch me!" Vander snarls, just once, before I lean close and brush my mouth over his. His lips are rough and scaled, with a hint of an old poppy on them. I kiss him.

Vander relaxes in my hold, eyes rolling into his head. *Lustitia*, my mother named this. *Judgement's Kiss.* Reserved for the worst and most delicious secrets. I open my mouth around his and suck out the blood-tangled untold. It slips from him to me, gliding down my gullet and into my stomach heavy-like, healing and filling me in a blink. Whole and delicious.

Sated at last.

My chelae retract. I release Vander; his head thunks to the floor. Limp.

"You killed him?" Aben asks into the silence.

I wipe my mouth with the back of a sleeve. "See for yourself."

Aben eases out from behind the bar, still holding the meat cleaver at the ready. His eyes don't leave me as he bends to check for a pulse. When he finds it, he blinks and his gaze breaks away as he runs a hand over the smuggler's chest, feeling the rise and fall there. "He's alive."

I snort. "I'm not a murderer."

Aben's cleaver drops to his side, forgotten. "What did you do?" He stares at me, searching. I smirk, it's not often I'm met with wonder. But I suppose Aben has seen enough this night to look beyond fear.

"I ate him."

"*Ate* him?"

"Him and his secret, everything that made Vander who he was." And come morning he'll wake as a blank slate. He'll never regain those memories. They're in my gut now, slowly digesting. A fresh start for a feed.

There's a humph from the stairs and a pad of feet crossing the saloon. Freda leans over Vander's sleeping form, pursing her lips. "Good as dead," she says at last. Then she lifts one foot and swings it hard into Vander's side. I wince at the crack of ribs breaking. Freda spits, straightens her tunic and turns to us. "My thanks."

I finger the bullet hole in the gut of my robe, frowning at the dried blood there. I'll have to get new clothes in the next town.

"You really can't stay?" Aben asks.

We're back in Roper's field. Dalziel and Freda are building a bonfire of herbs and bracken to calm the bones once and for all now that their murderer is gone. Dalziel practically dances as he does it. He is free, his daughter is returned and, if my hunch is right, they've found a new hearth to share at Macey's farm.

The widow watches Dalziel and Freda work, holding a bunch of lavender to throw on the blaze. A faint smile plays over her lips.

"No," I tell Aben. "Secrets to find, souls to eat and all that." *More wicked magic to hunt. It's never ending.*

As if sensing my thoughts, Aben produces the two halves of the spell book and gestures it at the fire. "Can I?" He asks. "I mean, is it safe to? I'm not going to get cursed, or jinxed for all eternity?"

A snort escapes me. "You won't," I assure him. "Without a wielder it's just a book. A dangerous book." *As for how Vander got his hands on it, that's a secret I'd like very much to know.*

That's the frustrating thing about secrets. They might nourish me, but they don't reveal the inner workings of their creators. The same way a person will never know the mind of the cow that became a steak on their dinner plate.

We sit together, watching the pages curl into ash until the bonfire burns low and the sun breaks over the grass.

Aben stands, still in his toe-holed sandals from Dalziel, and holds out a hand. "If you must go, know that my door's always open," he says. "Don't be a stranger."

I take it. His grip is firm, yet warm, and a pang echoes through my gut. Emptiness of a different kind. Funny as it may seem, I've come to like this rag-tag crew tonight. "You know," I say, slowly. "I might just hold you to that." A grin creeps across my lips. "You better have some good secrets to spill when I come back."

Aben grins. "Count on it."

About the Author:

Nikky grew up as a barefoot 90s child in Perth, Western Australia, before moving to New Zealand in 2016. By day she works as a professional content writer and by night authors speculative fiction, often burning the candle at both ends to explore fantastic worlds, mine asteroids and meet wizards. Her creative work has appeared in magazines, on radio and in anthologies around the world. Her debut novel, The Rarkyn's Familiar—*a dark tale of a girl bonded to a monster—will be published by Parliament House Press in 2022.*

You can find her online at:
W:nikkythewriter.com | T:@NikkyMLee | F:nikkythewriter

WE BRING BALANCE

Stephen Herczeg

Air streaked past Daria's face, stretching the skin into a rictus grin. Thick goggles protected her eyes, but the padded ridges pushed in, bringing their own pain. Leaving the helicarrier far above, Daria's frail body, protected only by her kevlar suit gained speed as the Earth's gravity dragged her towards it.

Her target grew in her vision far below. An enormous alien object blocking out more of the ground as she approached, its immense size floating above the coastal waters, ignoring the laws of physics.

The Visitor, as it had been dubbed, arrived on Earth four weeks ago. People were split between terror and welcome. The nations of the Earth sent envoy after envoy. All manner of communications was attempted, to no avail. The object remained silent.

Leading scientists concluded that the Visitor was benign. A relic from space that had found its way to our shores like flotsam from a deep-sea wreck. Scans revealed no life within the object itself, and further examinations confirmed its composition of non-terrestrial metals and alloys.

The arrival had one main effect, an almost universal cooperation between all nations to begin an understanding of the strange guest. Whilst the craft hung above the Pacific Ocean in silence, conversations were had around the world. Multi-national committees of scientists and diplomats were formed to discuss, examine, and formulate plans. Arguments broke out in the United Nations over ownership, stewardship, and custodianship. Some discussions bringing rival nations to the brink of war.

The science community wished to study the artifact, many proclaiming that such an object was only the work of a collective effort, one which should be embraced by the countries of the world. Business groups pleaded their case to exploit any of the non-terrestrial alloys or technology on board. Some religious fanatics proclaimed the object a test from God, while mainstream proponents rejected their views as against the sanctified word of God.

While the people of Earth discussed and argued with each other over all things concerning the Visitor, it sat hovering. Silent. As if observing all below.

Then the Visitor moved.

One moment it floated above the waters of the central Pacific. The next, the East China Sea off the coast of Shanghai. The Chinese Government reacted without waiting for international sanction or provocation from the object. Ships were deployed and planes took off, arranging into attack formations. All waited. Ready for any sign of aggression.

A lone missile launched into the cloudless skies above the Yellow Sea. Its destination: the Visitor. Finally faced with an enemy that they felt had no chance of retaliation, the North Korean military acted. Their long-range missile delivered its nuclear payload as programmed.

The waiting Chinese military vehicles that survived the blast witnessed the horror that followed.

A beam radiated from the middle of the craft, straight into the heart of Shanghai, the most populous city on Earth. Within seconds thirty-four million people were vaporised, the cities of Nantong, Changzhou and Hangzhou following in its wake.

The rest of the world mirrored North Korea and retaliated with every weapon at its disposal.

When every last bomb, missile and nuclear device had been expended, the world held its breath. As the smoke and dust cleared, the world knew the result.

Nothing.

Man's fiercest weapons failed to even scratch the surface of the Visitor.

The alien object had been on Earth for less than a month, almost gaining acceptance of its presence. Within twenty-four hours it had written itself into legend as the most devastating event in the history of the human race.

Then it vanished again, reappearing moments later off the coast of New York City.

That was when special operative Daria Locke was scrambled, flying into the thin atmosphere high above and leaving the safety of her aircraft to plummet towards the Visitor. The arsenals of the world had failed to penetrate the object's armour, but the hope was a single soldier could succeed where weapons had not.

With metres left before being splattered on the hull, Daria deployed her anti-grav pads and pulled up for a gentle landing. The ship's exterior was a strange spongy material, almost like skin.

Daria looked up. Her HUD indicated the vent-like aperture that had been discovered by scans was close by. She sprinted towards it; her gait ungainly due to the malleable surface.

Squeezing through the opening, she found herself in a long circular corridor. Her helmet lights revealing walls made of the same porous material as the exterior. As she stepped deeper into the craft, the vent disappeared behind her, almost as if it was alive. She was alone, no light except for her lamps, no sound, save her breaths and thudding heart. A tinge of fear ran up her spine, she shook it away. This was what she'd been trained for. There was no time for fear.

The wall nearby opened, inviting her into an inner chamber. Stepping inside, Daria held her right hand forward, and toggled the glove to reform into a plasma cannon. Her orders were clear, this was not a diplomatic mission. The US military wanted this threat neutralised not befriended.

"Welcome Daria Locke. You have been chosen as witness."

Daria spun, searching for the origin of the voice. Moving the plasma cannon across the interior of the dark room, she found no obvious source and dropped her arm.

A bright light burst from the middle of the room. Daria raised the cannon, ready to fire. A nagging sense of fear grew deep in her mind. Even her training techniques struggled to quell it. She toyed with firing the gun and ending the confrontation, as the command formed in her mind, the voice spoke once more.

"You have no need for weapons. Only your senses."

Daria's eyes grew wide. Questions formed in her mind.

Did it know I was about to fire?

"Who are you?" Daria demanded instead.

"We are judgement," the light replied.

"Why are you here?"

"You called us."

Daria baulked. "What?"

"Your collective conscience. The minds of this world. Called out to solve their problems."

"What problems?" Confused, Daria's mind turned first to rage. She raised the gun and stepped forward. "You murdered millions of people. What problems does that solve? Why would we ask you to do that?" she spat.

The light flickered, hypnotic and cold. "Because your world burns. The land screams. The populace wails."

I don't understand. What has any of that got to do with your attack? The North Koreans attacked you, but you killed all those people in China. Why?"

"We do not care for your weapons, they are harmless. We were called by your collective conscience, so we have started the process. There are too many of you. Humans have become rapacious. Consuming too much of this world. Leaders talk, but none listen. We listened. We came. We will restore the order we once imposed. Those we removed were just the first."

"I don't understand."

"This is our return. A thousand million revolutions ago, we came. There were others here. Larger. Intelligent. They were of the same mindset as mankind."

"Dinosaurs? You're talking about the dinosaurs. But they were just animals."

"No, those you name were primitive. There were others much more ancient in time. All evidence of their presence was erased. The world became pristine once more. The plants and animals flourished. The Earth regained its balance. Then your species evolved to this point. We are here to act again."

"But you can't kill everyone!"

"We won't. Not this time."

"Will you kill me?"

"No. You must remain. To bear witness. To spread the knowledge to those that we allow to live. We do not wish to return again."

"I can't. I won't."

"But you will."

A large section of the far wall became transparent, showing the wide metropolis of New York, teeming with life. As Daria realised what was going to happen, bile rose in her throat, threatening to pour forth. Her shoulders slumped, her legs turned to jelly and she dropped to her knees as the tears began to flow.

"No," she cried, "You can't. My family is down there."

"Then bear witness. Balance will be restored. Spread the knowledge to others."

The beam of light lanced out from the ship, piercing the heart of downtown Manhattan. A cloud of white light flowered, devouring everything.

Daria stared. Her eyes wide. Her heart pounding. Tears flowed down her face as devastation replaced the light. "No! No," she shouted. She dragged the gun up and pointed it towards the light, it felt like a hundred tons to her devastated mind. "I'll kill you." Her mind gave the command to fire. Nothing. Daria dropped the gun arm to the floor, collapsing and sobbing. "You killed them all."

"And you were our witness."

"You're nothing but murderers."

"No. We are not. Where there is chaos, we create order. Where there is injustice, we bring balance."

About the Author:

Stephen Herczeg is an IT Geek, writer, actor, film maker and Taekwondo Black Belt from Canberra, Australia, who has been writing for well over twenty years, with sixteen completed feature length screenplays, and numerous short and micro-fiction stories. Stephen's scripts, TITAN, Dark are the Woods, Control *and* Death Spores *have found success in international screenwriting competitions with a win, two runner-up and two top ten finishes.*

He has had over fifty short stories and seventy micro-fiction drabbles published through Hunter Anthologies; Things In the Well; Blood Song Books; Dragon Soul Press; Oscillate Wildly Press; Black Hare Press; Monnath Books; Battle Goddess Productions; Fantasia Divinity and Deadset Press.
A growing number of his Sherlock Holmes and H.G. Wells inspired tales have found favour with Belanger Books and MX Publishing.

He lives by the creed "Just Finish It", and his Mum is his biggest fan.

You can catch Stephen at his Facebook page:
https://www.facebook.com/stephenherczegauthor

INVISIBLE SCALE

Kel E. Fox

It took a millennium for the world to stop burning.

First we fought the flames with water bombers and hoses and more fire. Then we turned and fought each other with guns and steel torn carelessly from the earth, as if by finding someone to blame we could put the fire out. When there was no one left to fight, we huddled in the ash and desert scars and cried. It no longer mattered if we'd set the fire ourselves, or if it had been caused by some other catastrophe.

I dreamt that one tree survived the inferno, one that hadn't been there before. A tree that walked unburnt among the embers, with a voice that carried clear despite the blowing smoke, and its survival seemed less strange to me than its ability to move. But we put more trust in visions and foresight now, never again forsaking the future.

I find it in a shallow valley of rare, black soil and I put my hand to the smooth-rough bark of the tree. "Great Tree," I ask, feeling silly, "why do you not move anymore?"

An eddying breeze ruffles us both, lifting my hair and shivering the silver-green leaves above me.

"I used to roam the stars," the Great Tree says. "Now I stand here so you may roam the Earth."

Light and shadow dapple my skin as the shades filter down to the rich brown of the valley floor. Did I imagine that immense, solid trunk shift under my hand? "But why?"

The wood-creak voice is soft as a whisper, tremendous as a spring storm wind. "I heard your cries. As your planet was cast out of the universe, I stepped into the rift. I breathe that you may breathe. My roots reach deep into the magic of the universe, that you may reach deep into your soul and perceive."

I bury my bare feet in the soft, pulpy earth, lean back against the trunk of the Great Tree and gaze up, past the glinting leaves, out to the sky. Towering clouds dwarf us both. An unspent storm, escaped from the winter past, threatens the horizon. It had been a butter-summer start to spring, and the universe always seeks balance on some invisible scale.

We are all made miniature under the late winter sky.

About the Author:

Kel E Fox ran an apothecary in a past life, was a stage technician before she finally embraced writing in this life and hopes to be a wizard in the next. She writes an eclectic mix of speculative fiction and is working on her debut release Darkhaven, *the first of a YA fantasy saga about a girl who gets struck by lightning, develops superpowers, stumbles into a global conspiracy and meets an alien god all in the same day.*

Kel lives in Perth, Australia with her life (and ballroom dancing) partner, two lazy cats and a wilful young Alaskan Malamute named after Nighteyes.

See more at <u>kelefox.com</u> *or find her on socials @kelelizabethfox*

Eternal Peace

Jo Mularczyk

Working for God is never easy; the long robes constantly getting caught underfoot, the eternal daytime, the unrelenting harp music. What I wouldn't give to hear a simple guitar riff or a melody tapped out on piano keys! Or a raised voice. Who knew that perpetually muted tones and whispers could give you a headache? Well at least the memory of a headache . . . the no-pain clause takes care of that.

"Gilbert! We've got another one," Lucinda stage-whispered to me in her (you guessed it) *angelic* tones. A document had appeared in her hand and she was now waving it at me with a look of awe. Lucinda had the uncanny ability to look officious, even when perched on a chair formed of clouds. Others lounged on sofas, nestled in beanbags, or swung in hammocks, but Lucinda had chosen to conjure herself an office chair. I had often been tempted to conjure a throne for myself but some shred of humility, and a not insignificant fear that this may be frowned upon, had stopped me.

It had been a slow morning lolling around in the area I'd derisively nicknamed, 'the outer office' upon learning that even Heaven has admin. I decided to energise the group.

"I'm open Lu!" I jogged backwards, calling for her to pass me the documents. At least I had planned to jog backwards, what I actually did was take one step, catch my foot on the hem of my robe and go tumbling gracelessly across the cloudbank.

"Gil, you have wings, use them man." Russell urged me with an exasperated shake of his head.

I brushed my hands over the front of my robes and stood up with as manly a flutter of my wings as I could muster. Russell's hearty laughter followed me as I flew over to Lucinda and sheepishly retrieved the file.

"You're a card," Lucinda muttered in her motherly way.

"You love it, Lu," I mocked as I retreated to a nearby courtyard in search of privacy. It was refreshingly deserted, and of course, beautiful. To my endless annoyance, all the cheesy cartoon depictions of Heaven were somewhat accurate. Clouds, sunlight, rainbows and decidedly Grecian-looking architecture were the reigning themes. The level of interactivity took some getting used to though, and the effect for someone prone to indecision could be dizzying. Right now, the clouds in the courtyard swirled, reflecting a kaleidoscope of colours as they formed and re-formed to mirror my thoughts. I concentrated and a small pillar appeared. With a sigh, I leant against it and opened the file.

File - 981 105

Action - 41B - To be weighed in the balance.

Melinda Allcott

Age 67

I hated 41Bs almost as much as their ominous titles. Nauseating enough to think that I now held someone's eternal resting place in my hands without having it pointed out in such a high-handed fashion.

"To be weighed in the balance," I muttered scornfully.

A low rumbling filled the sky, so I swallowed down any further snide comments and flicked through Melinda's file. Teacher, tick. Mother of five, tick. Annual charity donations, school volunteer, blood donor, tick tick tick. So where was the downside here? Oh here we go:

. . . lost faith after her husband's death. Agnostic with strong atheist tendencies.

The immortal sin. Heaven forbid anyone allow uncertainty or doubt to undermine their faith. I—

Another crash of thunder interrupted my thoughts and I looked up; a black cloud was hovering directly above me.

"Oops, sorry. Momentary lapse into mockery, derisive thoughts and a hint of blasphemy. My bad," I finished with a wry laugh. The cloud dissipated as quickly as it had appeared. I've never met the big boss man, but I sometimes think he gives off a distinctly Orwellian Big Brother vibe.

Closing Melinda's file, I stood and headed to the Hall of Balance.

A warm breeze ruffled my wings and robes as I walked. Just gently of course. The breeze was of the precise strength and temperature to be predictably and maddeningly pleasant.

"Morning, Gil!"

"Hi, Gil!"

"Enjoying a nice walk there, Gil?"

Cheerful greetings were being flung at me with the regularity of rifle volleys. I returned fire when I wasn't quick enough to dodge them.

A choral outburst from the east signalled a new entry through St Peter's pearly gates. Josie would be busy with the new initiates. Poor sods. I still remembered the heady cocktail of feelings—disorientation, fear, joy, relief. I shook my head to clear the memory and decided to take a detour past the Viewing Chamber. Maybe a hit of nostalgia was what I needed to shake off this funk. Just a little peek to see how they were all doing down there.

There was a long queue to get into the Viewing Chamber. Parents hoping for a glimpse of their children, husbands and wives checking in on their loved ones, teachers looking in on favourite students. They all just stood there so serenely, completely unbothered by the wait. Even if I weren't on my way to the Hall of

Balance with my 41B, I couldn't bear the thought of standing there for hours, caught up in all that infuriating patience.

I walked on until I arrived at the Hall of Balance; an imposing building, reflective of the weighty task undertaken within. I smiled to myself. Passing under the enormous golden archway, I fought the urge to roll my eyes at the ornate golden scales adorning the doorway. The appearance of a personal stormcloud was annoying enough outside, but having one lingering above you inside was mortifying. Experience told me that an eye-roll was a sure way to conjure one.

I made my way over to the weighing station.

"Morning, Gil, do you have a 41B there?" Walter asked chirpily.

"Yes, Walt, they're the only files you deal with right?" I asked with forced cheer.

"Haha, yes siree, Gil. You've got that right."

Who would have thought eternal cheer could be so exhausting?

"Is there anything you'd like to say first?" Walter asked expectantly. The first time he had asked me this question I thought it was his version of 'what's the magic word?' so I had offered up a cheesy 'please'. I had since realised that it was just Walter's way of putting on his game-face. He was acknowledging the enormity of the task we were carrying out here. It didn't sit easily with me, so I always declined the opportunity to speak. Not so my co-workers. I had been caught waiting behind many a lofty orator.

"Ok step up and lay the file on the scales," Walter offered.

Clutching the file tightly, I approached. I glanced uneasily at the statues on either side. Subtlety was not part of the design. One statue was a small set of golden wings, the other a leaden pitchfork. With a final deep breath I placed Melinda's future on the cold metal plate in the centre. It rocked and teetered and started leaning toward the pitchfork. This was my only chance, Melinda's only chance.

I summoned all the wonder I could.

"Hey Walt, is that a vision of the big boss on the glass window behind you?"

"Where?" Walter asked breathlessly as he turned around. I inwardly cringed at the juvenile prank, but that's the thing about truly good, pure beings: the complete trust.

I quickly placed my hand on the scales, tipping them towards the wing statue. A small bell sounded from the scales just as Walter turned back with a disappointed look.

"I can't see it. Not worthy enough yet I guess," he gave a self-deprecating shrug.

I felt a momentary pang of guilt. "You know what, I think it was just the light shining on a smudge. Sorry. If anyone's ready for a vision, it's you Walt."

"Oh well, maybe one day," he said hopefully. "In the meantime it looks like we'll have another lucky soul joining us." He nodded towards the scales.

"Well done, Melinda, I knew you had it in you!" I crowed.

Walt's smile faltered just a little, unsure how to respond to my humour.

I gave him the biggest grin I could manage, the type of smile that would have copped me a look of suspicion where I grew up. "Ok Walt, well I'll leave Melinda's file with you to process."

I left the hall feeling righteous. Well, except for the lingering guilt for deceiving Walt. I savoured the guilt a little, it diluted the righteousness enough to make it palatable. Besides, a little guilt was worth it for saving a soul, right? A good soul. Maybe slightly lost, but undoubtedly good.

"Hello Gilbert," a quiet melodic voice rang out behind me.

I swivelled in surprise to see Gloria.

"Hi Gloria, I didn't see you there," I spluttered awkwardly.

"Come and sit with me," she said softly. She turned and walked towards a small marble bench without waiting to see if I followed.

I followed.

We sat together on the bench. I rubbed my nose as cloying floral scents assaulted me. The offending flowers curled around the archway above our heads. I stifled the urge to roll my eyes at the architectural style of choice around here.

Gloria was breathtakingly beautiful. I couldn't describe any one feature though, she was lovely in the way a sunset was lovely, it just was. Ugh, this place even got into my thoughts and made them poetic.

"You have a troubled heart, Gilbert. A kind heart, but nonetheless troubled."

I looked down at my feet, anywhere but into those shining, probing eyes.

"You helped Melinda Allcott," she continued. It was a statement of fact, there was no question in her voice.

"She didn't deserve to be turned away because of a crisis of faith. She'd led a good life and then, because of one decision made in response to a tragedy, she was going to be punished." I wiped my face in frustration, surprised to find it wet.

"I can see how our judgement can appear harsh."

I nodded, surprised at her candour.

Gloria continued with a hint of sarcasm. "I'm sure our people can appear too cheery at times, our breezes too pleasant, our archways too . . ."

"Arch?" I interrupted with a laugh.

"Gilbert, we promised you eternal peace and you have not found it here. We believe we can help you in another way." Gloria rubbed my back, and I felt a tingling sensation.

I turned to see my wings had vanished. I looked at her in alarm. "I don't understand. You're kicking me out? You don't mean I'm heading to the other place do you?" I was overcome with a numbing terror. "You know I don't like the heat . . ."

"You will go back to Earth as a guardian. Your true calling seems to be to help the 41Bs. You can guide them as they face each crisis of faith."

"What am I, like a fallen angel now? Like Lucifer?!"

"No Gilbert, calm yourself. You will walk again among the humans. You will appear as a spiritual advisor to them. Humankind will be facing a trial soon, one that will threaten their way of life and undermine their relationships. It will lead to crises of faith, spirit, identity and wellbeing. Its reach will be unprecedented."

"Not your best sales pitch, Gloria. I mean you're really frightening me, what are we talking about war, pestilence, plague? The bible's greatest hits?"

Gloria looked back at me enigmatically. Her eyes conveyed a deep sadness that scared me more than her words.

"What can I do?" I whispered.

"Humankind is strong, resilient. They will overcome. But they will need those like you to guide them. Our only requirements are that you not spend too long in any one person's life and that you not approach anyone from your own human life. If you ever decide to return, you need only speak the words."

A warmth like liquid light spread through my body. "What is that?" I asked in wonder.

Gloria placed a hand on my now wingless shoulder. "Joy, Gilbert. Go now and find your peace."

I closed my eyes and waited for my after-afterlife.

About the Author:

Jo enjoys writing in different genres for a range of audiences. Her stories and poems appear in magazines and anthologies including The School Magazine's Blast Off *and* Touchdown; One Surviving Story *by* ICOE Press; fourW thirty's New writing; Pearl anthology; Wonderment *by Poetica Christi; Zinewest publications;* Short and Twisted *by Celapene Press; several Storm Cloud Publishing anthologies; Daily Science Fiction; the US magazine Cricket;* Fire Burn, Cauldron Bubble *by Bloomsbury UK; several Black Hare Press publications and other upcoming anthologies.*

Jo loves to share the joy of writing through delivery of creative writing workshops and as mentor to a gifted and talented student writing group. Jo is an author with the Littlescribe student literacy program, providing story starters and writing tips to students who go on to co-author the stories (www.littlescribe.com).

Jo lives with her husband and three children in Australia.
Website: www.jomularczyk.com
Facebook: www.facebook.com/jo.mularczyk.author
Instagram: www.instagram.com/jo_mularczyk_authorpage/

The Competition Between Good and Evil

Barbara Smith

In the beginning

the war unfurled,

merciless swords slashing

on a blood-soaked land,

until day and night were of equal length

a red moon and sun observed

glowing side by side.

Good magic and evil,

in parallel worlds

Once contained by the scales of justice,

now represented by

a multifaceted doorway in a hollow room,

where I stand with bloodied hands.

The once level transit system is now twisted

into a roped chandelier the underworld cannot reach,

which I stand beneath,

watching light dance across stone walls

as if looking through a kaleidoscope.

The weary souls of the dead,

that once stood erect,

balanced and equal,

have become contorted, frozen objects,

sharing intimate

raven coloured embraces,

between hero and villain

A thick mist blows southward

through the cavern opening,

enveloping those, barely living,

in the bloodied leaf litter,

seeking truth

within godforsaken destruction.

The time traveller

disguised as a warlock,

begins his descent

A distorted coloured vision,

THE COMPETITION BETWEEN GOOD AND EVIL

from his maddening castle,

disrupting the deathly gathering.

He waves his staff high in the air;

the dead begin to rise.

The pure of heart who still breathe,

unable to fight back

despair at the desolation

Watching from her Elysium field,

 the virgin takes the hand of her apprentice,

eyes sunken and despairing.

They walk the spiral stairway towards the Warlock,

 to lead the song of judgement.

 Crimes of defilement

 will be revealed,

within the ranks of the dead,

as the apprentice places his feather

upon the golden weigh tray

the virgin carries.

The end becomes the beginning.

In a perpetual cycle

until balance can be forged.

About the Author:

Barbara has worked in teaching at Universities for many years and published her debut picture book, Otis Paul & Harry the Hairy Echidna *in 2019. Having tried her hand at many things, from spinning wool to building an earth house, she now illustrates children's stories, writes in varied genres, and spends time with her beautiful family. You can read her collective poetry on her blog* <u>Lifeandbeyondblog@wordpress.com</u>, *where she adds some skills as a photographer. You can follow her on twitter @BarbAnn.*

ADRIFT

Brianna Bullen

The photo reformed, pixel by pixel, until she was there on the glass. The red rose in her hair formed last, lacking all acuity at first, and morphed as a bloody smudge behind the ear. With her curly hair and fur coat, she looked like a retriever who had been sprung running through a rose bush. Instead, she had been sprung smuggling an old lady off-world for medical treatment. Lines of determination were cut deep into her face, particularly by her mouth; she's wearing years that aren't her own. Animation takes the years off, but forced into straight line neutrality, nothing distracts from her unaugmented skin. It's as browned as a paperback left in the sun. I touch the lines, a flicker of a hand movement really, a slight caress. I don't know the impact this face will have on me before pressing down on the button.

This was the first photo I had ever seen of the woman in faux fur, splashed like a watermark against a skyscraper on my way to the embassy. Upon registering my interest, my optic system instantly brought up the seven hundred and thirty-six stories related to the woman. Mai-Sue Evergreen. It projected the feed out from my glasses in a colourful mix of click-bait headings and hyperlinks, highlighting the people walking past (most wearing vintage Mickey Mouse ears, coming back from neo-Disneyland) in blue.

I scrolled with blinks, before shaking my head and back-tracking to my favourite journalist's take. People smuggling, arson, invading a hunting gala to free the robotic animals, general subversion: fifteen to twenty years, expected. A familiar name had taken on her case. A particularly smug git of a lawyer I had crossed. Radio static memory invaded my present: "You hurt me, so I wanted to hurt you back." Memory, delete.

Even from the beginning, my ex-love and my new love would be inextricably linked; past and present and future, and future-past smearing together to create a potential fate.

I did not get my visa to GJ 1132b approved; I didn't even get one to Mars. I didn't expect to, but what else was there but dreams and delusions to keep you going in 2101? Smog hung thickly over the skyscrapers, like a pullover rotting and falling apart at the edges.

I am there, and then I am not, waking from my past. A copy/paste consciousness. All I can do is return to my working script, memory minimised. The ship looks down at Earth. Although I know I am moving onwards, pin-balled through space, everything feels still. It may just be the silence affecting my perception. There's the sound of thought which sounds like a game of Minesweeper, just tapping messages, fluent in Morse and in coding, to be sent out into space. I imagine seeing the letters pulling away in zero gravity, having only each other for company. They know they will never reach their destination—do they even have a destination?—but continue in their lonely journey.

The image of earth on the window flickers. It's faint at first, and then a jagged 'Z' of pixel fragmentation carves up the image. I click the window, and the image of Earth disappears. Beyond, space stretches out, infinite and unresponsive. The dot in the distance, white and pin-head small, looks like a constricted pupil. The button I must press is shaped like an enlarged version of it; I look away from the screen to see it mimicked on the monitor. I press it, once every ten minutes as required.

I don't know why I press this button.

I don't know why it can't just be automated.

Maybe that's the true meaning of punishment: meaningless repetition.

But I press it anyway, without fail. Sleep is my only reprieve from white circles; I allow the black space to swallow me. I am primed to sleep for six minutes, to wake with time to prepare. I never quite enter REM. But I'm always alert, pumped full of artificial stimulants. REM sleep has become a dream in itself. Instead, I am left to darkness and the dim impressions of memory.

The dot is the planet I orbit, name undecided when I left earth. I am off-world, but not 'off-world' in the conventional sense; I am not entering Mars. I am further than any man or woman or being from Earth has ever been. I've outdone Russell the Labrador; he died just a few thousand kilometres behind where I am now. It must have been so lonely. I imagined him licking the picture of his owner, reported to have been put on his desk, before succumbing. It is such a lovely thought. He died billions of light years away from the astronaut he had been taken from, never knowing his purpose for being so far from home.

The anthropocentrism I apply to his last moments is too sentimental. Something conjured for human comfort and not reflecting actual reality. One of the few messages I received was commemorating his fate on his anniversary death-date. The other was that they had decided on 'Asimov' for the name of my planet. My dad's voice appeared, and it took a whole bottle of emergency rum they had included for direct download to the IV to remove the aftertaste of the dad joke: "of all the sci-fi authors they could have selected, Ass-imov was truly the right partner for Uranus."

ADRIFT

I was curious about the woman, Mai-Sue, so I kept an eye on the trial. This wasn't hard; the press coverage made any new findings ubiquitous in conversation. In my spare time, I examined all her social media postings, trying to uncover a simulacrum of the woman in family photos, holiday snaps, and tagged posts, but what was initially made public displayed a surprisingly conservative woman. Her activity logs, including anonymous postings and personal chats, were made transparent after conviction in accordance with Article 66366b, and they displayed a truly remarkable woman that quickly dominated contemporary folklore. The most interesting posts were compiled and became a best-selling eBook, topping both the true crime booklist and the general reading list. Those pertaining to her agreement to 'assist grandma with her road trip' were anthologised.

I read and studied the text as gospel.

My sister sent me message after message, and even tried to call me a couple of times. I missed her surrogate birthing her child.

My right arm itches like it is infested with mites. There are two tubes embroidered through it: the tube below is keeping me hydrated, the tube hooked in above is feeding me liquid nutrients. Today it is a cloudy blue liquid, but at times it is brown. The insert holes are now permanently open in my skin, like wall sockets. The door to my room opened and a figure stepped in, the first other being I had seen in three years. I said hello and attempted what I could remember of conversation. Even when I realised it was a robot, programmed for this one function, I kept speaking to it until the regulator had been fixed, and sleep restored.

My stomach pricks with pain and dead weight when I regain consciousness. I groan as I press the button, drops of sweat building from pain and exertion splattered over my face. My mouth is coated in the bile of a bad sleep. I clutch at my stomach, feeling the stretch of all my cords and hooks, my skin tugging apart to accommodate their stretch. I instantly know what is wrong. My colonoscopy bag has torn; I am leaking shit, thick and unpleasantly repugnant as off Vegemite, seeping through my fingers as I try to hold the bag together. It's agony; as though I'm bleeding out, losing my entrails through a gash in my stomach.

My mind floats to happier places, rose-tinged and with the seeping consistency of fairy floss. They're pleasant for now, but they will give me pain if I do nothing but consume them. I'm back to where I first met her, at some gala in a place made of marble and poor taste. A pair were racing drones, narrowly missing the ancient chandelier. My first thought, when I saw the criminal celebrity across the room giving me a curious stare: I should have worn a nicer shirt. I couldn't choose my bartending uniform, though.

"Here's to lighter sentencing in exchange for media spectacle," I saluted her with a flute glass. I took note of her bodyguards-slash-jailors, grey glasses firmly in place.

She smiled and took a sip of her own drink, stance open but casually indifferent.

"How long have you been out now?"

"Two weeks."

"You're the reason for the paparazzi outside."

"Were you expecting something different?"

"I was quite hoping it was for myself. I mix a fine long island iced-tea."

She smirked and took a sip from her glass, a drink longer than her face and just as cloudy. She was drinking to get drunk, possibly to forget. "That you do."

"How was prison?"

"I'll tell the press about it before I tell a stranger."

"Fair call. I just have one question."

"Is this an interrogation?"

"Something like it. Was it worth it?"

She looked exactly like her mugshot, determination a setting she could switch on and off. "Every second."

She moved to turn away from the creep bothering her. I can't say I blamed her. My mouth was looking for syllables but not even taking in air. But I'd been wanting to talk to this woman for months. Something about her face, the details of the case—

Gaps in the coverage, something not adding up.

"Whatever happened to the old lady?"

She stopped mid-step and swivelled like a clothes-rack. "That's the question, isn't it? The one that hasn't been asked."

"The one that should've been."

"All that talk of human rights, of morality and ethics—and the person at the centre of it all, the person who needed the questions to be asked, isn't included in the question at all. Know why that is?"

"You sound like you know the answer to your own question," I said. "You're very obsessed with justice for a convicted human smuggler."

"Because it's easier to talk about justice in the abstract; remove the actual human element and focus on the 'criminal' and the moral quandary. Treat a person as a victim, they get spoken for; treat a person as a victim in the abstract and they're silenced completely."

"Careful. With that level of self-righteousness and coherency they might throw you back in the slammer."

"Or allow you to become a lawyer," Mr. Whitley, the man working on her defence said as he walked up behind her, PR mode in place.

"Why? Because they haven't drained it out of me?" she was back in the conversation, a verbal pugilist, out looking for a fight, before she lost the argument by giving in to self-reflection. "Although I guess making me a spectacle makes me lose track . . ." as she did of her thought.

When I next wake up, the hole has been patched up—no, I realise the bag has been removed entirely. In its place is a new piece of metal, pulsing and warm to the touch. A dual functioning system: bladder and bowl. I feel their pistons powering through me. The words "Thank you" don't come as easily as they used to, but I release them like a prayer to no one. With a second thought, I tap out the message on the keyboard. "ThankyouthankyouthankyouTYTY" until I lose all feeling in my hand. I hear it thud off the keyboard, registering its loss of functioning in the split second before my consciousness completely goes under.

My persistence to get to know her paid off. She recognised that I wanted to get to know her and not just her case. "A far cry from most assholes these days."

We went to a zoo, a place for scientific curiosities and the few remaining animals, outside of pets. It contained only a few species of 'livestock,' reminders of the barbarity of the process of execution and meat eating. I went only once before for all the loneliness it contained, and the bleating of the single lamb meant nothing to me The creature's larynx moved, through its ugly teeth came an awful shriek, but the sound was audible pollution. I knew not one word; it could not touch me. A man in a fancy black suit and sunglasses complained as he stepped in the waste seeping out of the sheep stall, He swore until he was purple in the face that it would be a good thing if the animal just died out. Mai-Sue took a sip from her overpriced shake and then chucked it by his feet, allegedly aiming for the garbage.

During our date, Mai-Sue said something to me in a language I've never been able to decipher. It runs through my consciousness from time to time, as if it will unlock something in my past or in my future. It was in reference to my attempts to learn another language in her presence, repeating the phrase after every word on the app and getting excited whenever I heard the success bell. All I heard was "pavlova," and it made me long for sugar and eggs.

Being tone-deaf feels like a life sentence.

I wake up. Thirty seconds to get reaccustomed to my body, ten seconds to press the button, and another minute twenty to get reacquainted with the beauty of space. If I want to, I can generate images over my window to prevent its sublime terror from getting in. I spend a minute watching a cat video—the classic of the little grey kitten raising its arms in surprised surrender—before the drugs kick in to take me back under.

I wake up, I press the button. I go under.

I wake up. I press the button. In the last twenty seconds I've become aware enough to scream.

I go under.

I wake up at 4:20am, so eager to see the sunrise from the balcony again that my body refuses to let me sleep, a beehive of excited internal processes. It takes me a moment to realise I should be thinking 'I woke up', the fabric of the memory so warm and comforting I refuse its past tense.

Mai-Sue is asleep by my side, Bruce curled up and asleep over her heart. He needs a constant beat to sleep. As if sensing my gaze, the apple-headed dog raises its snout, blinking eyes awake. They're little watery black pits, shining with intelligence.

He watches me watch her, scrutinising me in the way dogs do, as if verifying you are where they left you and not going to move anywhere, before yawning and laying his head back against her chest. Traces of food poisoning from a dodgy burger gives her face a greenish hue, and I fear she may be literally dead to the world before she lets out a thudding fart.

Her twisted pose seemed uncomfortable, but the snorts and snores sounded peaceful. I left the bed, padding to the kitchen to get myself and Mai-Sue a glass of water. I place one glass by her bedside, then take my glass out to the balcony. The sky is dark grey. The car outside the opposite building is vomit brown. A colourless morning. With nothing to see and still heavy with sleep, I pad back inside. Slumping into the mattress face first, I promise myself just ten more minutes.

I missed the sunrise.

I wake up, expecting the sunrise. All I have is the stars. Space looks like it is being viewed from underwater. Dimly, I think the stars remind me of eyes waking from sleep—Mai-Sue's or Bruce's, I'm not sure which.

The tube in my left arm is extracting blood millilitre by millilitre, purifying it through rudimentary dialysis. Multiple regulatory assemblages, which pop like a metal patchwork quilt embedded in my flesh, are keeping my organs and artificial parts in check. The one in my chest deposits immunosuppressants into my system every twenty-four hours. Every one of my biological functions is displayed on the screen beside me. I watch their minute changes because my mind is too groggy to even feel them. I need the numbers to reconnect me with my body. A green spiked hill is constructed on the screen, a steady drawing equating to 79bpm. It is only on seeing this linear rise and fall that I can, however faintly, make out the rise and fall of my chest.

There is a full body simulation taking up the left third of the screen, reconstructing the flow of blood and various systems' processes, from kidney to blood pressure to my pig's heart rhythm. Even though it's painful to arc my arm beyond the regular forward button press, I reach over and click my lungs, enlarging them on the screen so I can see every simulated inhalation and exhalation, all the way down to the capillaries and their dilating blood vessels. It's morbidly compelling; as though I am watching my own internal ghost. My brain scans show a slowing down of functioning; I can see the medication slowly release through my system.

The smog was getting worse, causing emphysema. I got my results over the phone. My coffee was sprouting three larger bubbles that looked like eggs, hatching milk. I imagined boundless spiders spreading like a stain over the surface, until they were over the rim and dropping onto the carpet. I blew the imaginary creatures away, playing it off to Mai-Sue as if I was cooling the coffee down, and not letting my imagination run away on me.

She looked at her hands, the raised skin and raised scars.

My own were coated in haptic sensors to increase their ability to feel during sex, and to increase my typing speed.

I look to the hands pressing against the buttons: all their augments have been stripped out. I wear the scars like regret.

She told me sometimes about prison, speaking like an automated machine. We were in the café, talking over cigarettes, coffee, and Bruce's whines, when she is back in prison. The main punishment is repetition and isolation. The tasks they were given were uniform drudgery. Then her words became louder, clearer, stronger, more familiar, and while I knew she still wasn't with me, she was no longer back there . . . Moving to practical considerations helped. Funding would be better spent on rehabilitation and utilizing each woman's unique skill set, or so she argued.

"We have minds. We've fucked up, royally, often without any option of atonement. How can you overcome murder? All those seconds of memory, all those connections, all that life gone at your hands? How can you turn back the clock on subverting the law? Deciding you know what's right. We can't take back our crimes. But some of us could change for the better, if given half the chance. What they do to us is torture, not reform. Experimentation in how far the body and mind can bend before it breaks. Trust me, you don't want to wind up in there."

I'd heard it all before and was too tired to agree in words.

Repetition, I realise, is complete drudgery. I hit the button with a punch and tear out my blood regulator. Why am I doing this? Why haven't I questioned it?

This is Capital punishment, with a capital C-section. I will my legs to move, and when they don't, I look down at them, half expecting to see sewn-up stumps, pus-filled and bedsore ridden. But they're fine, though limp and lacking muscle definition. They're like two matchsticks stuck awkwardly onto a diorama,

about to snap off. My brain sends a message 'move, twitch, lift.'
The left foot jolts, hypnic jerk hurting, before I fall unconscious.

I went with Mai-Sue to help collect rubbish from the beach. The
little commodified patch of land looked like a postcard;
umbrellas, hotels and sunbathers in colourful assembly lines. All I
had wanted was an excuse to walk across the beach with her. Her
hair was dyed red at the time, so it must have been just before—
just before what exactly? Things ended. How did things end? I
scroll through memories, but all I find are corrupted files. So back
to the beach. By the time I'm back in the scene we're further
along the beach, in the tucked away place 'barely anyone' goes. It's
the 'authentic' experience: a ticket stand sits among the dunes,
limiting the walkers to thirty a day.

She stops to look at driftwood with the consideration one
would give a museum artwork or the latest technological gadget. A
flock of terns scuttle across the sand. The movement is so natural
and life-like, that only the stilted twitch of the one bringing up the
rear betrays their animatronic nature. The birring whir chirp
sounds like unoiled clockwork turning. The sound soon gives way
to the lapping sucks of the ocean swallowing the sand and our
crunched footsteps. She always had quite the pace, even in sand—I
don't think I really caught up with her once that day. I was
impressed by her tenacity in that present; enthralled with her past
but was trying not to show it. She'd drawn a line so that I'd

understand: she wanted to live with no reference to the person she had been. Not because she was ashamed, but because she was tired. All the questioning, all the attention for what she thought any human being would have done—it was completely destroying her faith in humanity. An impossible task, forgetting yourself, if ever there was one, and I told her so.

She picked up a six-pack plastic ring, black market non-biodegradables for the edgy nostalgist. "Fucking disgusting." Impaled into it, a fish wriggled like a notification, guts sprawling slowly down the plastic.

"It's okay; I don't think it's real." I pointed to the exposed wires, minute and networked.

"Those are veins."

"I think that's highly unlikely. Veins in a fish? Not since the twenty-first century," I teased, lifting up my incinerator to remove all traces of the plastic and organism in one neat zap.

"If there's no hope, there's no point." She looked out across the ocean. "Which reminds me: how did your latest off-world application go?"

I inhaled the air in a saline swallow. "I feel like I got closer this time."

When I next come to, I'm delirious. I feel like my body's dried up. Every cell is cringing and creaking. My lips are chapped, for the first time in however long. I accidentally tear a strip off in rubbing them. I hit the button and ponder my next minute. If I remove everything, will the induced sleep stop? I doubt it. But I could run, get as far away as my weak legs can take me before any alarm is signalled. Does the ship even have alarms? Shit. Focus. Decide. I rip everything out that I can: the IV hooks, some of the external sensors. Some are still inbuilt, fused. It takes a second for my blood—turgid black goo—to ooze from the holes in my arms. I'm reminded, however distantly, of a childhood spent with playdough strainers. My blood pressure drops acutely—I don't need a monitor to feel that—and I'm not sure if my next sleep is from the drugs or hypotension. It feels like a victory.

"So what happened to the lady you tried to save?"

"They gave her the life-changing treatment, of course. Just, not the life-changing we wanted."

I didn't like the haunted look in her eyes when she said "changing".

I ease through consciousness, in and out, and barely manage to press the button. It looms, doubles, and disappears before pulling back together into the one image. By the time I get over my vertigo, more than two minutes have passed. The body has a funny way of altering your perception.

A body lie—bodily experience that disguises the reality of pain—is better than the alternative.

*

"They then shipped her back to earth with an express ticket to The Retirement Village."

I blink awake, weak and malnourished, unused to surviving without the steady flow of nutrients, but I imagine I'm growing stronger with every black out, just like I imagine the planet is growing closer with every one of my drastically limited Circadian rhythms. I blink to make myself more awake. I blink. I blink.

I blink: Mai-Sue's concerned, blinking too fast as she gets the call. "Bull-shit, bull-shit, bull-shit", she mutters. New details have emerged in her case. Prior smugglings, some espionage. She hasn't been taken back into custody, yet. But it is only a matter of time. "Fuck it. They're going to fuck me over like last time. Might as well go after them, see if I can unravel them a bit before they cut me to pieces."

I blink—

It was a stupid fight. By the rocks at the beach, Mai-Sue screams at my refusal to help hack the rigged Mars Transferral Mainframe. I want to do things the right way, even if it takes ten years. The world might be dying, but if our morals die with it then there's nothing left to save.

I tell myself not to hit the button. I will my hand to stillness. It shakes and trembles. My insides feel like they're being peeled back, bones extracted. Don't press the button. My breaths become rapid. I gasp for air. Will this kill me? How much oxygen is left on this ship? Don't press the button. A mantra: people used to have those, once upon a time, when clarity and meaning were still sought. Don't press the button. Just see what happens.

I press the button.

I scream.

They take me into custody. The officer smirks as I'm paraded past. Secret service? Have we been watched? Or is my mind just protecting me from what they've accused me of doing?

This time, I'm going to run. I'm going to get through the door. Maybe there's a long corridor; maybe there's an exit into space. I'll run through the corridor, my bones creaking, and burst through every door I come across. In each room will be another human being, lonely and gazing off into space, pressing on their own buttons. Mai-Sue will be there. Maybe Bruce, too, wagging his tail.

Whoever signed up to this . . . project? The brave and the excited, I think. From memory. From memory . . . They'll have the same dopey smiles, the kind of those blissed out on too much data, or nostalgia, code trickling through their veins and neural pathways until their augments and veins rupture from within. Take on too much of the world's information and it kills you.

I imagine the blissful shudder of the aneurysm of information flowing out. But they'll be right. They'll be fixable. Just as undernourished, under-exercised, over-doped, over-augmented as me, but capable of being unhooked. Once the withdrawal from nostalgia stops, we can take over the ship. Manually steer it. Faster. Brighter. Burning through the stars until we get to the planet.

Mai-Sue's arm is locked around mine. She's singing karaoke. It's the night before the beach, just after she got the call that she'd be sent back in soon. The 'Underground' was just as pre-packaged as the rest of society, with its own rules and regulations. Its own gaps to fall through.

I jump off out of my chair and regret it when my leg snaps. I'm panicking from pain and instant delirium; red and woozy behind my temples, red spouting from my leg. The bone is piercing through the skin. Oh god, oh god, oh god. In the past I'd say it ironically, but now I'm hoping someone's hearing me. Oh god. I vomit from the pain. Mostly bile. Acrid. Nothing in the belly. I want to pass out. I'm used to passing out but this—this is white hot agony short-circuiting my brain. But I just know that if I do, I might not come back. My innards might spill out like a bag being opened.

My hand clasps over the wound, trying to hold myself together, but it makes for a shit tourniquet. Who's going to press the button? Shit, I've made a mistake. I can't even see out into space. The ground's clinical-clean disinfectant infects my nose. Everything's burning. Why am I here? The ground is bulging and drooping in white spurts, the bile varnishing the Jackson Pollock pattern. I need to hit the button.

I wonder if it'll take me home.

I don't dream, but I hear Mai-Sue's voice, that sentence she said to me a long time ago in a foreign language. It repeats like an advertisement as the two robots—square little boxes on wheels with massive claws—reassemble me, squirting liquid numbing agent and disinfectant on my leg.

They insert a needle into my arm, but for once I don't go under, I'm just completely numb to it all. I watch them break my leg back into place, healing the skin with nanobots. It solidifies, not even as scar tissue but as completely healed flesh. They 'fuss over me' in the only way they can—treating me with the gentleness I project onto them. One turns me over and the other reinserts the catheters into me. It's done quickly. Not roughly, but with no hesitation either. The hesitation's what used to make me nervous. I miss it. I barely feel any pain from the reinsertion, but groan anyway, partly out of habit, partly to convince myself I'm having a conversation.

The monitors beep and steadily hum in response. I reach over to touch on of the robots on the head, feeling the warmth of its processor beneath, but it quickly turns and shuffles away. The other one remains, observing the monitor and looking over all my augments, upping the dosage of the sleeping medication. Closing my eyes, I superimpose the image of the friendly nurse, freckled and frazzled, who patched me up when I broke my ankle following a drunken dare on my birthday. I imagine I'm sucking on the green whistle, directing my own intoxication under her laughing face. Friends whose names have been lost to time, distance and indifference are standing by the entrance, petrified faces turning to laughter.

Mai-Sue's voice penetrates over them. There's a clock on the wall, ticking down (but to what?). Bruce is there, wagging his tail and whining. I wonder who's let him into the hospital and if there will be any complaints. He runs up and licks my fingers as I wake up in my own bed. Just him, nothing else matters. His eyes take up half his face, little black mirrors as wet as his nose. They reflect the universe. I let him crawl under the blanket and just let everything be; the world moves slowly, but I am at peace. In the background, Mai-Sue's voice, the old Russian phrase, repeats.

The words form on the blanket I hold above my head; first in Cyrillic script, repeated over and over. Then, over time, it becomes anglicised, until finally I decipher what she's saying.

Мы все собаки Павлова.

My vse sobaki Pavlova.

We are all Pavlov's dogs.

Primed for their torture.

About the Author:

Brianna Bullen is a Deakin University PhD creative writing candidate writing about memory in science fiction. She has had work published in journals including LiNQ, Aurealis, Voiceworks, Rabbit, Multiverse: An anthology of international science fiction poetry, and Woolf Pack Zine.

She won the 2017 Apollo Bay short story competition and placed second in the 2017 Newcastle Short story competition. Her manuscript was previously a finalist in the 2018 Subbed In Poetry Chapbook competition. In 2018, she was part of Nexus, an Arts Access Victoria collective for artists with mental health recovery lived experience.

THE DIVINE PRINCIPLES

Emilie Morscheck

Rinar couldn't understand how her original self died at Sorcerer Seus' Magic World: *Where all Magic is Real!*

Or hadn't died.

That was why the STASIS Corporation transport had dropped her off at the theme park entrance with the word 'Clone' tattooed on her arms and a tracker bracelet bio-locked to her ankle. She needed to prove that she was dead within two hours. If she wasn't, Rinar would be scheduled a prompt appointment to meet her maker.

The staff operating the turnstiles at the entrance were dressed in long robes and fake smiles. They ignored Rinar as she approached and forced her way through the gate. She didn't exist to them. If only her body were as insubstantial as a ghost.

On the other side of the main entrance, Rinar joined the crowd as it poured into the open mouth of a cave. Illuminated crystals poked out from every surface, all just out of reach of an injury lawsuit. Further into the tunnel fake smoke was pumped across the floor. Mystical flute music whispered from an unknown source in the rocks.

"Welcome to Sorcerer Seus' Magic World!" A voice-over echoed, repeating in a dozen languages.

Rinar hurried through, unable to work out why she'd been at the park. Her memories were last backed up twelve hours ago, and she died hours after that.

At least her death at the hands of a dubiously operated theme park was starting to make more sense.

Outside of the cave, the horizon was filled with rides and fake buildings, many spitting rainbow fireworks into the sky. The sweet and salty smells of carnival food made her stomach grumble, but Rinar wasn't allowed to eat. In the event of decommissioning and reconstitution, a full stomach made the process . . . messy. How easily they turned matter into a new body.

She checked the coordinates on her STASIS-pad of her corpse location. It took her towards a giant mobius Ferris wheel. Up-beat pop music blared from the speakers along with wooshes and zaps of magic.

The exact location she died was behind the staff only sign in the alley beside the Ferris wheel. Rinar paused in front of the sign. Her memory download finished. Her head jerked forward as the last bits of data rushed in.

She remembered then who she was. Rinar Hawthorne. Xenologist searching for the Zibanu Scales—a device the ancient

Zibani used to contact their home world. A device that operates on non-STASIS networks.

As her head cleared, her heart pounded. She shouldn't be at the park. She was leading the corporation straight to her discovery.

Rinar approached the alley and peered around the sign to see a vegetated space with a narrow path descending into the theme park's underground tunnel network. Why would a Zibani artefact be there?

She should leave. Her time was almost up. There wasn't enough evidence either way of her death. Maybe they'll let her live.

Before she pulled back, her legs were struck out from underneath her. Something clipped around her face, stopping her from speaking. Rinar's stomach dropped and tears wet the corners of her eyes.

"Hmmmm!"

Rinar was shushed and her hands were bound as she tried to struggle. Her attacker hacked at the tracker on her ankle, pulling it off and then dragged her to her feet. Rinar shook her shoulders but she was just pushed forwards, heart pounding so loud she couldn't hear anything.

All she could think was this was probably what got her killed the first time.

Rinar was marched down the narrow path and her world became even darker under the hood. Perhaps they didn't have a lethal weapon? Why else move her out of sight of the theme park crowds?

They walked for several minutes before the hood was ripped off. Rinar blinked against the lights aimed at her face. Her vision evened out.

"Shit."

Rinar was looking at herself. Rinar 1.0 rolled her eyes. "Took you long enough."

"What is going on? Why are we here?"

Her original self raised her arms to indicate the cavern that they were in. The walls dripped with moisture and real crystals grew out of the wall.

"Why hood me?" Rinar said.

Rinar 1.0 pushed her glasses up her nose. Her clone was the Perfectly-Reformed™ kind, not the Made-to-Match™ variety, and therefore didn't need glasses.

"I forget I'm such an idiot sometimes," the original said. "I can't have two of me up there. But I need two of me down here." She removed the bindings from Rinar's wrists. "I found it."

"The Scales?"

"Yep." She walked deeper into the cave, using her STASIS-pad torch to light the way.

The beam bounced over a body slumped on the floor with an oozing head wound.

"Who's that?"

"I had to make a clone somehow."

The ID chip was pulled from the victim's skull. 1.0 must have reprogrammed it with her own DNA ident.

She pointed the light upwards and Rinar saw what she came for. She expected a set of rusty scales but instead there was an old-earth style rotary phone wedged in the rock face. Two cords dangled down the wall.

"That's it? How does it work?"

"The Principles," 1.0 said.

Rinar nodded. "Of course." The Zibani had a way to convert lifeform energy into power. "So why haven't you tried it?"

"I have, but it takes two."

Rinar understood. She could be smart sometimes. The genetically identical Zibani pairs allowed for the lifeform to survive energy conversion. Without another word, they plugged themselves in, and Rinar dialled the universe.

About the Author:

Emilie Morscheck is an Australian author of speculative short stories and novels. While working on her first novel she found the time to study engineering and arts at the Australian National University. Emilie was a participant of the Toolkits Fiction program and a creative editor at the ANU's student paper Woroni. Her works on Wattpad.com have over 50,000 reads. In 2019 Emilie received an artsACT grant to edit her YA fantasy novel These Cursed Waters. *She is a fan of kelpies, selkies and watery graves. @EmilieMorscheck*

THORNE OF LORE

Cage Dunn

1.

The night sky faded. Damascena entered the amphitheatre as false dawn touched the Dividing Ranges. She grabbed the mallet and rang the gong. Once, twice, thrice. This had to be quick. The marauders were moving, and Damasc needed to get downslope.

Yawns and whispers rose to a rumble. The gathering villagers greeted neighbours, swore, asked questions. They glared at Damasc standing on the petitioner's block and pointed to the boy at her feet.

"What is that?"

"How dare she?"

"It's against the law."

Some spat in her direction. Some covered their faces or turned away, looked to the upper tier for an explanation.

Damasc created a bubble of gift-light. It didn't illuminate much, but if the sun rose over the outer wall and obliterated the wan glow before the Warden arrived, it was too late. She needed to return to duty, to stop the enemy destroying fields and farms.

The wooden mallet swung heavy in her hand. She wanted to ring again, but three called an emergency meeting, and any more cancelled it.

Two soldiers stood guard behind her. People whispered and hissed, told the soldiers to grab the mallet and end the travesty.

Shivers ran up the moon-vine that held the boy. He stared wide-eyed at Damasc, his almost naked body rigid with the cold. Damasc shaped a small glow of heat until warmth enfolded him. The villagers' response to him alarmed her. The disdain they displayed was no excuse to ignore the needs of the many. She glared at them. Their flocks and shepherds depended on Damasc.

And her dog. She didn't dare call him a dingo. Not here. The hunters would seek permission to trap and kill him.

Heavy robes swished in time to the steady slap of leather slippers. The Chief Warden emerged behind the chairs of law, fully robed, wigged and masked in gold. She stood in front of the central and highest chair until all bowed, then sat. The Warden's two Seconds came forward and folded the robes across her thighs. They bowed and returned to their places.

"This meeting is called to order." The Seconds rapped their staffs on the marble floor. "State your cause."

Silence settled.

"Do you think to make us wait? That will not happen, Guardian of the Passes. Why have you summoned the Council? What is it you bring before us? Tell me who keeps the people of Shaower safe while you stand here?"

"I wish to petition the Chief Warden for permission to train—"

"Is that what I think it is? Why is it still alive?" asked a Second, jabbing her staff toward the boy.

Rumbles filled the audience.

The Chief Warden raised her hand and the crowd quieted. "Where is your dog?" she asked. "Is it not part of the compact that your animal . . ." she looked down her nose and sneered, ". . . be with you at all times?"

Hands and shawls over faces didn't hide the titters or accusations of sleeping with animals, denning with dogs, and the stink of her hut.

The leader of the Military Sect, the man who threatened Damasc at every meeting, stepped from between the carved pillars. Vrath's flat black eyes didn't blink, but the rapid tap of his fingers on the hilt of his sword brought a cold breeze to Damasc's neck.

"May I be permitted to report?" Damasc maintained her forward focus.

The Chief Warden rubbed her facemask. "Report on the transgressors first, then explain bringing an enemy into our midst."

Damasc unclenched her fists. "Two groups of nomads," she said. "I followed the group that moved through the . . ." she debated whether to state which path, chose discretion, "low pass. They moved too fast for the illusions to hold. My companion followed the other group, to harry and frighten." Damasc lifted the boy to his feet. "I did not see this one. The dog sniffed him out."

Did the Chief Warden understand? Damasc bowed. "He was tangled in wait-a-while vine, and when I touched his skin, I felt it. He has the Gift."

A shudder went through the tiers. The Chief Warden rapped her staff. The noise stopped.

"The proof?" The Chief Warden spread her robes over her lap.

"The dog has vouched for the Gift."

"Oh, the dog that isn't here, the dog that can't talk, has affirmed that this enemy of the people has the Gift of the Goddess." She sniffed the air. "It isn't here, is it?"

"No, the dog isn't here," Damasc said.

"And yet you want us to take it on your word alone that this creature has the Gift that you cannot find in your own people?"

The crowd huffed.

"I will need to train him."

"When was the last test of our people for those Gifted?" a Second asked.

"I tested at the mid of winter."

"And you found no sign?" The Warden raised her head. The impassive mask slid and garbled her words. She pushed it up. "How many did you test?"

"All who presented were tested with no result. Not all with the Gift receive at the same age, and some are not strong until they use it."

"Why not test all the villagers?" asked a Second.

"Once a person is named, they cannot bear the Gift."

"And yet you capture this," the Second jabbed a finger toward the boy, "enemy, and choose him?"

"How many Guardians of the Pass do we have?" the other Second asked.

The Warden nodded.

"I am the last," Damasc struggled to keep her voice steady.

"Who is on duty while you are here?" the Warden asked.

"I am the last," Damasc repeated. "My mother died last summer. She begged for help to find Gifted after the deaths of the two Mentors the previous autumn."

"You are not the last. I would have been informed of the deaths of our Guardians."

"The notes were proffered and accepted, Warden. Each death notified. The Gift takes energy," Damasc straightened her back, swallowed the pain. "They died from exhaustion. With no time to rest or eat the body will fail." She squeezed her eyes closed until the burn eased. "I am the last Guardian of the Pass, and I am weary. I need to be at my duty every moment of each incursion. I require an acolyte."

"We will offer adequate coin to anyone who volunteers for training—"

"The Gift does not offer to those who choose matter over spirit."

"What utter idiocy you speak. It's guard duty, not magic. You watch and set traps, the dog assists you. Nothing to it. I move to dismiss this petition."

"I have the right," Damasc raised her voice, "to train those I find fit. The Gift has not been found among our families. None will even present for testing." She scanned the crowd of downturned faces, then returned her gaze to the Warden. Her jaw tightened. "I seek dispensation from the law, so I can train this child."

"Where is your dog?" the Warden sneered.

"He is the watcher of the mountain, not ours to demand his presence. His pack is—"

"Now it's a wolf!" The audience giggled at the Warden's comment.

"In the mountain way, every dog is a wolf at heart." Damasc pulled the boy close to her side. "The bond we share is for a limited purpose. It is not to burden him with other demands." And he'd been too wary to come near the village. "The dog is of the mountain, and his rules for the Gift—"

"Oh, the magic again." The Warden nodded her head until the mask slipped. "It's for fools and idiots, and Guardians, it seems. There is the Law for us all, and the teaching Lore for children, and no magic is required."

The crowd erupted with a cheer, until the Seconds pounded their staffs.

The Chief Warden tapped her fingers on the arm of the chair, scanned the audience tiers. "It is an enemy you bring to us, and we have laws for our enemies. Do you know our laws, Guardian?"

"Yes, Warden," Damasc conceded. "Yet the boy is a child, and the laws do not apply."

"He looks old enough. Why do you call him a child?" The mask slipped further, showing greying hair and sallow skin behind the mask.

"He is not yet named, and therefore, a child by our laws. Which do not permit a child to be judged as an adult."

"He is the enemy. The sentence for any transgression, any knowledge of our home or our ways . . ." the Warden adjusted her mask and glared through the holes, ". . . is death."

"He is Gifted, and without assistance, there is no protection from the marauders."

"The enemy is death. Death to the enemy!" The Seconds chorused the words, repeated by the audience.

"He is Gifted! The first since I undertook the training for my role. I am the last, and without assistance, there is no protection from the marauders. Our justice, meted through the written laws, determines our humanity. The laws apply to those who are of age and capable of studying our histories and judicial writings."

"We apply our laws to our own," one of the Seconds said. "Our people, not those who threaten our ways."

"The child is close to maturity," the Warden added. "He is an enemy. The law stands. Put the prisoner into the pit to prepare for execution at dawn."

The sky to the east burst into red splashes on the rising mist.

"I object." What else could she do? "I request a full hearing."

Gasps erupted in the tiers, followed by silence. All eyes turned toward the petitioner's block.

"All stand," the Seconds chorused and banged their staffs. The crowd stood, eyes lowered as the Chief Warden spread her arms. A staff was placed in each hand by the Seconds.

The judgement.

"We have heard entreaty from the Guardian of the Pass to spare a prisoner, an enemy captured from within our lands. We consider it unwise to allow petitions that dispense with legal rulings." The Warden brought the staffs to the front, clasped them high. "As the Chief Warden of the Council of Law, I render judgement on this matter." She smashed the staffs to the floor. Sparks flew. She repeated it twice more.

"The sentence is thus:

"The laws do not allow a child to be sentenced to death. However, this one is near maturity and would be an adult but for one ritual. Whatever our intentions, in good conscience, we cannot put the axe to his neck.

"Therefore, our decision is that the boy will be taken by the Guardian and presented to the One True Goddess, our Lady of the Lake, as an offering." The Warden placed the staffs to one side and sat.

"That's as good as a death sentence." Damasc kept her voice small, but there were no other sounds. Her mind panicked, tested the options she could have taken, but she was already an outsider, barely tolerated. If she'd kept him on the trails and trained him, the sentence would be death by axe to the neck the first dawn after discovery. For both.

"It is an offering, Guardian, and if accepted, we pray the One True Goddess will gift others and renew her blessings to Shaower," one of the Second's said.

The Warden raised her arms. "Duty to the law is duty to justice. You are bound by our laws, to our justice, and through your service, to the One True Goddess. You will take this enemy to the Lake and offer him as sacrifice. You are under oath. Do you understand?"

Damasc nodded, her teeth clenched. The lump in her gut burned like flame. "Who will guard the paths from the marauders?" The words came out scratchy. "Who will protect the village while I undertake this errand? If a Guardian is not on duty, the secret paths aren't hidden. Lives are at risk. Farmers, hunters, gatherers."

"We have soldiers. We have shepherds. Many are there capable of setting traps. We will ensure our safety." The Seconds moved to flank the Warden. "We may even find we no longer need the improbable magic you seek."

It was over. A death sentence by any other name. Blood sacrifice wasn't in the Lore Damasc read from, wasn't in the teachings from her childhood. They were terrifying stories from those who were captured and brought to the village as workers, but they were stories, tales her mother told on dark, moonless nights. Now the Chief Warden had written the terror into the Book of Law, denying the Lore of the Goddess.

"I will leave at dawn," Damasc said, bowing.

"You leave now. We will not have the eyes of an enemy see the preparation for rituals of the spring equinox, nor those who will receive their true names at that ceremony."

A soldier raised his arm. Damasc tightened her pack and grabbed the boy.

"I do not require an escort. I am a Guardian of my word and will undertake to follow the orders lawfully given." She turned her back on the Warden and strode from the amphitheatre. She didn't look back.

2.

The lake was inland, west, where the sand-cyclones blew white death into the foothills. Damasc had never travelled inland. Guardians of the Pass didn't have the leisure to travel.

The armed escort left her at the gorge leading to the low pass, with a warning to be gone by sunset. The sun was already sliding low to the west.

At the first bend of the path, Damasc grabbed the boy and pulled him into a shrubby grotto. The dingoes howled in the lowering darkness. Damasc opened her senses. Tension filled the air like a looming thunderstorm. All the creatures were silent and alert. The best and fastest route to the west, through the path below, sparked with alarm.

It felt wrong. The animals felt it, Damasc felt it.

Do not enter, Dingo's howl warned. *Traps, soldiers. Death awaits the unwary.*

High walls, dark passages, twists and turns in the path. An excellent site to set a trap. Dingo's vision showed her the hunched backs of soldiers. Looking toward the village. Facing in, not out.

An ambush. For her.

Thank you, my friend.

Why did they let her leave with the boy if they considered him so dangerous? Damasc agreed to undertake the task, and she would prove her dedication, but that they didn't trust her rankled. She'd find a way through the mountains to the west. Damasc had her mother's stories, the mind-maps, mud-maps, song-stories of the moods and movements of the mountains to guide her, but nothing else. If she was lucky, they'd make it off the mountain. Not far or fast in unknown territory, and even if they made it to the foothills . . .

She closed her eyes and visualised, prayed her memories of words and song were good enough to find the border of the mountains and what lay beyond. And if she did? If the Goddess was fair and just, she'd hear the plea from a supplicant.

First, she had to get through the mountains. Alive. And with the boy.

The Dividing Ranges separated the harsh wind-tormented ocean from the inland. The secret Paths of the Passes were the teachings of the Guardians, passed from Mentor to Guardian to Acolyte, unbroken. Until now.

The marauding nomads fought vicious battles to get from coast to inland, and again when they returned in the season of sand-cyclones.

Did we not warn the Guardian? Dingo howled from a different direction, his voice twisting in the shapes of the gullies and variable breezes. *Come to the high boulders where fat moths den.*

Damasc pulled the boy to the ground. He gathered sticks, bundled them.

"No," she said. "Not yet. No extra weight."

He frowned, and Damasc tilted her head toward the path. "Look to the rocks there," she said, and puffed a breath into his face.

The black shadows within the dusk-darkened rocks huffed white puffs. Breaths.

The frown deepened, his eyes widened, hands flew to his mouth.

"Yes, a trap. Tonight will be dark. A late moon. We wait." She crossed her legs and leaned against the stone. "The dangers of the mountain are worse than the threat of soldiers." She pulled out a fruit leather. "Here, eat this."

The boy grabbed it and stuffed it into his mouth.

"When I tell you, go there," she indicated the steep face of the cliff above them. "There's an overhang. We can't stay here. Too close to the path back to the village. We wait there until they leave." She rummaged in the pack until she found the knitted woollen hat and a spare shirt, tossed the bundle to him. "Make sure your breaths are small, and if you need to, roll down the hat to cover your face. There are eye-holes."

The boy slid it over his head, unrolled the rim, and clasped his hands before his mouth, shoulders hunched.

"Are you cold?"

He nodded.

"There's nothing I can do about it now, but keep your hands and feet warm. As long as you can feel them, you'll be okay. Once we get past the soldiers, we'll light a small fire." She peered into his eyes. "Okay?"

He nodded.

"You don't talk much, do you?"

He shook his head.

"Can you talk?"

His body stilled like a trapped animal. "Yes. Sometimes. When there's something to say."

"Okay." He had a voice. It was a start. "Rest. Lie down if you want. I'll keep watch."

The dingo rustled his arrival in the low scrub beyond the grotto. *Enter?*

"There's a dog coming in," Damasc said. "He's my bond to the mountain, and he won't hurt you."

The boy's eyes widened, and he leapt up.

"Quiet. Don't frighten the other pack members. He is my friend, but the pack is wild. They fear the large that move too fast, and chase those that run. Sit."

He squatted in the way of the nomads; shoulders hunched into his neck.

"Enter," Damasc whispered.

The first touch of Dingo's padded paws on dry earth set the boy to trembling. Dingo sniffed at him, sat his haunches on the ground, and wagged his tail until the white tip blurred.

"Food?" Damasc asked.

The growl from Dingo's stomach was his answer.

The boy froze.

Damasc held out a piece of dried tack on her palm.

Dingo snatched it and chewed.

Why pup fear?

"You're a creature worthy of fear and respect."

Boy is one with us. Hears pack.

"What?"

"I hear them," the boy said. "I fear."

Fear not, boy. Not I. Another has chosen you. The words you hear are whispers, not growls. Be calm. Be wolf in mind and body.

"I don't understand." Damasc held her hand palm up. Dingo came forward, head down. She rubbed his chest, his ears, scratched his back. "How did a pack member know of him, yet you did not? Or is there more to the story?" The dingo pack had their own rules, and Damasc wasn't part of the whole. Dingo chose her as a companion for his own purposes and wouldn't share unless she became pack.

It is pack. One has chosen him, marked for her own. She is Alpha.

"Is she here to take him now?" Would that solve the problem, or make it worse? Duty to Shaower and the law of the Goddess, or duty to pack and the mountains?

Pack calls. Come with pack. Be wild, be safe.

"I can't, Dingo. I am bound by honour to the duty."

See trap. He sent her another vision of the soldiers. Not one or two. Half a hundred soldiers, all armed. Spears that stank of venom, shallow holes that didn't hide the stench of their spoor.

"So many soldiers for a Guardian and a boy." With that much spoor, they'd been there since early in the day. They must have left the village immediately after her petition that morning. Lain in wait while the escort took her the long way, 'to ensure the boy didn't recall the paths.'

Yes. Come to pack, be alive. Be free.

"I seek the Goddess and the justice of her word. I cannot run free." The first time Dingo offered her pack was after her mother died. He'd told her pack wasn't blood alone. "I am not a wolf, Dingo."

Wolf at heart. Run and hunt, howl and den. Be one with inner wolf. Come now.

"I can't, friend. I have obligations. I have duty." What happened after, if she survived, was a thought too far. "I thank you. I thank the pack, but I must complete my task." If she followed the quest to the end, and there was a Goddess, would she sacrifice the boy? Was there another way?

A puff of dust, a flick of tail, and Dingo was gone.

The boy fell backward, yanked the hat off his head, and stared at the shrubbery. "Did you hear him? He offered you freedom. Let's go with him," he said.

"Us?" She shook her head. "There is nothing to consider until duty is fulfilled."

"Duty to what?" he crawled to the edge of the hide and peered down-slope.

"Duty to the Gift, duty to the people, the mountains, to my mother. I have given my oath of loyalty to the Goddess." And her mother's teachings. Not the same as the Chief Warden's Law.

"The soldiers—what about their duty?"

"They are not a problem. Not for me. You have the Gift, boy, but can you use it? Do you know what you can do with it?"

"This journey was for my initiation. Then I'd hear the stories, then I'd have known if it was real. If . . ." his voice faltered. "I have to be initiated first, to know if I bear a true name and a true Gift. These stories are forbidden to those not named in the true way of the Goddesses."

"There is only one True Goddess, one Lore," Damasc responded without thought. "The stars are hidden. We move now. Up, go up." She pointed to the dark smudge of the slight overhang halfway up the cliff face. "You go first, I'll be behind you. Here," she pulled out a short rope and wound it under his shoulders, around his chest, and secured it to her waist. "But don't fall. It will make noise." She lifted him past the first outcropping of rough stone. "Grip with fingers and toes, don't try to hug the mountain, move sideways, one hold at a time."

Forty steps later, she regretted the rope. He fell twice in the easy section with good grips, three times after he'd chosen slippery holds. After that, Damasc showed him the places to grip, when to hold, where to move. Her back ached, her stomach muscles burned. There'd be bruises all over her body tomorrow. If the soldiers didn't pierce them both with arrows before then.

The overhang was smaller than she remembered. The kid shook like a cornered tree quoll, his blue hands tucked into the shirt as far as the elbows. Damasc pulled him into her chest and held him still. Her body warmth would help, but the strength of his Gift blasted at her senses when he was in contact. Why didn't he use his Gift to save himself?

"Are you hurt?" she asked through gritted teeth.

"My foot," he said.

"How bad?" She didn't want him screaming in pain, but her efforts at healing took time and more moon-vine than she had.

"I could walk, if you need me to." He curled into her lap, his small body light but rigid.

"Relax. I won't let you fall. I need my hands to set the illusions so the soldiers don't see us. Hold me, but don't move. Okay?"

He nodded.

Mist dripped from the overhang. She caught it in her hands like a web, expanded it, shaped it into a cloud of dense fog, thickened it with vapours of snowmelt. It rolled down to the lowest points, settled on the path through the ravine. Voices drifted in the thick blanket, muffled.

". . . missed . . . gone . . . wrong path . . . too late . . ."

Damasc wrapped her arms around the boy and smiled.

What would they do next? Patrols. She'd know who led them by the direction and shape of his searching. As long as it wasn't Vrath, she'd choose a low path and slip past them. Then the boy wouldn't need to climb again.

If it was Vrath, it was a kill order from his mother, the Chief Warden. Why else waste the best soldier on duty to the west, with the marauders in the east.

Either way, it didn't matter. It wouldn't stop Damasc. The laws came from the Goddess, as did the Gift. Justice must prevail.

The fog eddied. Every shift of vapour through the shrubs and gullies showed where the soldiers were placed. All low down the hill, flanking the path so that she'd be deep in the trap before they sprang. Suspicion confirmed. Vrath's strategy, his pattern. No way through.

3.

Just before dawn, Damasc led the boy upward. The path was impossible for anyone carrying weight or weapons. They reached the jagged ridgeline without incident. A sliver of moon gave no light. A new moon would rise with the equinox, two days hence. A good omen, she hoped.

They moved fast, not slowing until they reached the western edge overlooking the flat-topped hills.

She pointed to the lightly treed grassland at the junction of two ridgelines. "That's where we'll stop," she said. After that, the ridge descended between the flat clearing and two paths and led almost directly west. It was rough ground, and they'd need to be rested.

"I can't." The boy slumped to the ground and curled up. Within moments, he had slipped into a deep sleep.

Change of plan. Damasc covered him with her coat and put the pack under his head. She slid to the edge of their refuge and scanned the paths behind them. No sign, no sound. A few animals, not alert or alarmed. They weren't being followed. Yet.

What about the boy? The coat wasn't warm enough. He was too skinny. Damasc gathered sticks and small stones, then made a small fire to keep the boy warm while she harvested water from trees.

By the time the sun warmed the gravel under her feet, she had enough to fill two gourds.

"We have to carry water from rivers and wells," the boy said. "How do you do that?"

"I can't always get to the river." She gave him the smaller gourd. "I take water from trees if it's safe. Otherwise, I dig."

"Can you show me?"

"No. We're sacrifice. If we survive the journey, and the lake, and the Goddess, things may change. Right now, we don't have time." She gave him the sack of leathers. "Eat it, and I'll fix your foot."

The boy ate every morsel and licked the last scratchings from the pouch. He drank one mouthful of water and offered it to Damasc. She shook her head and continued working the last of the moon-vine over his injury. The bleeding had stopped, the wound a deep scrape from the cliff falls. Bad bruising, but that required plantain, which only grew in the lowlands. She stitched the spare set of soft boots over his feet.

"Ready?" She hefted him up and waited while he adjusted the sheepskin boots.

He nodded.

"Follow me. It's a tight track, but don't look down, and don't fall. I won't be able to save you this time." She tied the rope around him again, fastened it to her waist.

The goat trail at the highest point of the ridgeline was narrow and slippery. Damasc held her arms out for balance as she negotiated the thin crest. The boy copied her but shook so badly the rope around her belly tugged her off-balance.

"Tell me about the nomads," she said.

"Can you teach me how to heal?" he asked, the trembling down to a mere shudder.

"It's the same answer as the water. Nothing changes until after the Goddess hears the petition. Tell me about your family."

"How can I learn about the Gift if no one shares what they know? What if it—" He squealed.

Small stones under his feet pattered down one side of the sheer face. His foot slid out, his arms flew wide. Loose stones rattled, rocks split away, fell, cracked open on other rocks and thundered down the slope. The boy's face disappeared in a cloud of dust.

Damasc pulled at the rope, hauled him up through the deluge.

An avalanche roared, tore hunks from the path.

"Get on my back!" Damasc turned. The kid jumped on. She grabbed his legs and pelted along the crest, refusing to look to either side as the ridge collapsed beneath her and slid away.

Downhill, too fast, dangerous. Nothing to stop the momentum. Damasc bounced from moving rock to solid stone, which then shattered. She jumped, leapt, bounded. Dared not slow or think. The lower trail wasn't any safer or wider, but it had more solid stones. Steps that didn't disintegrate when she touched them.

Too fast. She gripped the boy tight, used his weight to tilt for balance, to hurl them faster until the dirt remained solid under her feet.

When the grinding settled, when she reached the base, she let the boy down. Damasc gulped air, leaned on her knees to catch her breath. Listened.

The dust cloud sulked along the gullies and ravines, drifted with the breeze. She'd missed the path that would take them over the flat-top. The boy handed her a gourd. She filled her mouth, swirled the water, swallowed it. More dust flew above the crest. Damasc scrambled to look over the top.

Shouts rumbled in the mix of rocks and stones. Boots thumped, fear screams rolled in with the booms.

Damasc's heart pounded. She glanced to the north.

Soldiers scrabbled to get up the incline opposite. Forty men in black uniforms. Pointing up. At her. The best archer in the village couldn't make the shot. Too high, the wind from the avalanche too unpredictable.

Vrath showed his frustration in the way he forced his soldiers up-slope for a better shot.

Damasc scrambled back to the boy. "We have to go around," she said. "We missed the best path." She puffed a few times. "Through that cleft." She hitched her head that way. "Between those two." The weathered hills were the end of the mountains.

Her mother's stories didn't go beyond the foothills. She'd have to rely on the boy after that.

"Where is the lake?" she pulled him onto her back.

"Which one?"

"What do you mean? I want the lake of the Goddess. Where the Lady of the Lake sees petitioners." The haze over the plains beyond the foothills was heavy and thick, blanketing. "How many are there?" Her calves cramped with the changes in terrain. As soon as it levelled out he'd be walking, injured or not.

"The lake of the Lost Souls is where I'd be initiated. That way." His hand showed the mid of north and west. "There are other lakes. Salt lakes. There's no fresh water. No one comes here except to make offering to the Goddesses." He grinned. "And a line of salt lakes from north to south makes a barrier that saves us from the mountain people stealing our land."

Salt? Did they farm salt?

"Why do you come here?"

"The herds."

"Of what? What lives out there?" She gripped the twisted tree trunks and slithered down the south facing slope. The wrong direction, but it was easier going, and the angle of the next valley led more west.

"The lakes are the boundary. Inland are flatlands, grazing, animals that move from north to south as the grasses grow. We open the water holes, dig out any that collapse. It's safe enough.

Not alone, though. In the desert, there are no storms, no slavers' boats, no need to hide."

"What about the sand-cyclones? Aren't they storms?" Damasc wished Dingo were here to keep watch for the soldiers. The terrain didn't give her any safe high points for observation.

"The dust storms come in late summer. The animals go north to the marshes. They give birth and get fat, but we can't go there. Venomous insects, huge snakes. The ground is wet everywhere except the sandbanks—where the crocodiles nest. We go back to the ocean, to fish when there are no pirates or slave-traders. They don't risk the winter storms of the sea."

"Why not stay in one place?" Damasc lifted him over a tumbled wreck of rocks. The ground levelled out, but still more south than west. "Can you walk now?"

He tested his ankle, limped along the rough track. "To starve in the desert? To be captured by slavers on the coast?" He swallowed a mouthful of water as he walked in front. "Your people may own the passes through the mountains, and we may have to risk our lives to get through, but those risks are nothing compared to some." He winced when his foot slipped on a loose stone.

"Why were you in the mountains? It's early for travel, isn't it?" Damasc called him back and put him on her back. She stood for a moment, listened, heard nothing unusual. The boy didn't seem to know which path to choose. It would be up to her to find a way out of the mountains. Which way would be fastest? And what would Vrath choose? He'd know these passes, he'd have the advantage.

"It's for the ceremonies. This year, my family gathers the herbs and seeds. Presents the gifts." His stomach rumbled. "Gather food."

"Are you hungry? Can you wait?" How much did he know of the area? "What foods are near the lake?" Damasc increased her pace. She was used to carrying weights for long distances, but now she had to find food for two while also keeping ahead of Vrath.

"There's no food there. Unless you want to get sick." He sipped from the gourd.

Irregular trails led down. Damasc chose the ones that cut across the hot red rocks rather than the shaded paths. The air was different, the dryland forest crunched under her feet. Spindly trees hid nothing, offered no protection.

They reached the base of the mountains. Soon her feet were on flat land. Behind them were low foothills. The mountains hovered far behind.

"We're here," the boy said, and slid from her back. He wrenched dry grass and rubbed his legs and arms, pulled off the boots and scraped the grass over his feet. Red welts joined the black bruises on his ankle. The waft of a strange herb filled the cooling late afternoon air.

"What's that?" Damasc asked, although the information wouldn't end up in her herb-lore.

The grass he used looked and felt like spinifex. She ripped a hank and rubbed it over her forearm. It hurt. She dropped it and turned to the west. Haze. Everything was sharp white. Hard breaths of stagnant water rose into stark shapes, mists floated like the dust of marching armies. Harsh salt stung her nose. Underneath the swirls of salt and haze lay a lake. Somewhere.

When the air cleared with a gust of dry wind, she saw it.

Not one lake. Many lakes. Hundreds of lakes. Large, small, indistinct, part-full, near-empty, glassy. All crusty with salt.

"Which one?" Damasc ran to the foam-edged shoreline. "Which one is the lake of the Goddess?"

The boy shrugged and walked out from under the tree line. "No idea," he said. "I don't know which Goddess you're talking about. We have the Virago, the three sister Goddesses. Warriors and fighters." He kneeled at the edge of a stinking estuary and bowed. "May the Goddesses protect those in their care." He spread his arms wide and lowered his forehead to the sticky mud. "May those in the hands of the Goddesses feel the blessing of their touch and be gladdened." He maintained his position for several long puffs of the stinking, muddy water.

"Get up," Damasc said. "We have to find the right lake."

"There is no right lake. There are all the lakes, the whole system. The lost souls wander these places, and the Goddesses protect them." He pushed himself up. "There's the place I know for the ceremonies. It's a long way. That way."

What do I do? Damasc closed her eyes. To the north, where he pointed, was all lake. To the south was all lake. She imagined the sounds of the mountains and forest behind her, felt the influence of calm. It was lost as soon as she opened her eyes. "It's supposed to be one lake, the lake of the One True Goddess. I need that lake."

"Why?"

"Honour binds me. I seek a judgement. And then I can return to my people with the obligation fulfilled, justice meted. Even if it isn't what they expect."

"I don't understand."

"Nor I. But take note of the words spoken by those of the Law, and see around them to find more truth than fact."

"You sound like my father when he's preparing for a testing. Is this a test?"

Damasc couldn't answer that. "The Goddess is just. We believe she created our Lore. We must abide by her words. We are bound by oath to her writings."

The sight before her, the flat white shimmer of so many salt lakes, made a lie of the words in the books of teaching, where there was one lake.

The boy looked at her strangely from under his eyelashes, as if she was an injured animal.

"Why don't we camp over there?" He nodded toward a promontory that jutted above the water.

Damasc followed him, dragging her feet.

This wasn't right. When she'd made her commitment to the Gift, she'd made her oath to the Goddess through the words of the Book of Lore. That book was indisputable, written by the Goddess. But her mother's book was written from memory when Guardians were no longer given access to the teachings. Her mother's book included her maps and recipes and the ways of the mountains. The memories of her mother's book led her here, which was where the map indicated the shoreline of a lake.

Damasc's heart weighed heavy as an icy cornice on the peaks during a blizzard.

4.

The mist on the lake wasn't like mountain mist, the water didn't answer her entreaty. Twice she flourished the request for shaping with her hand over the surface. Nothing happened. She didn't understand the nature of the salt haze. It was heavy, and fought her attempts to move or shape it. She was vulnerable without the illusions. Tears burned her cheeks. She swore and stamped when it failed the third time. When the boy held her shaking hands in his and cried with her, Damasc stopped trying.

She set up a place to rest, drifted close to sleep, but the strange environment startled her to alertness. Nothing was familiar. The night sky was so wide, so distant. So vast that it stopped her breath. Dark, and yet alight with millions of stars. No clouds, no rattles of trees, no clatters of stones moving downslope. No animals, no birds, no insects except the voracious mozzies and midges.

It was too quiet. Alarming.

Each time she sat up, the huge expanse of emptiness threatened to overwhelm her senses. In the mountain forests, the world was limited, bounded by solidity. Out here, nothing broke the sense of forever. She could walk to the horizon and beyond, on and on past this world and the next, and not see a living soul.

The lakes shone with the reflection of stars. Ripples spread in a slow pattern that didn't feel fluid. A surface lined with black wavelets, a constant movement too slow to see. She looked back at the mountains. Breathed them into her body, spread her arms to enfold the sense of them. Black shapes flecked with glistens of snow, sharp contrasts between wooded slopes of shadows and black gullies and crevices.

Home.

She wanted to go home. There wasn't much there for her, but she had duty if not family. Purpose, if not acceptance.

The boy shouted in his sleep, his cry carrying far. Damasc kneeled and placed her hand on his head. Warm.

"Don't call the soldiers to our camp."

"The pack comes."

Damasc stood and tilted her head, listening for the calls of the pack, or even a single note of Dingo. "I don't hear anything. Is it just your dog?" Was he lying? Maybe his people were close.

"Don't they like being in the open?" His head turned toward the south.

"No. Danger lies in being easily seen by those who hunt you." She ranged out with her mind for Dingo, put her hand out to keep the boy silent.

"Aren't dogs the hunters?"

"Every creature eats, therefore every creature both hunts and is hunted. Shhh."

"Oh. Anyway, the pack waits."

In tree cover, in safe places, Dingo and Damasc communicated with movements and noises that weren't out of place. Out here, exposed, the sounds carried. She understood the reluctance to emerge.

Come, Dingo called.

The Gift in her blood sang to hear his voice, but Damasc didn't see him, didn't sense him. The perception of the world blurred to wild shapes, mirages. Instead of shadows, it was reflections of light within pale hues, but not illumination.

"I can't find you," she whispered.

We wait in the dark. Come to where water meets stone.

One promontory had scrubby shrubs growing near rounded boulders, the salt water held back by the dirt washed up against them. Damasc looked deep into the shadows, saw the reflection of his eyes. She set off, bounced from firm ground to firm ground, avoiding anything too flat or too shiny. Salt and bog, a new experience.

As soon as Damasc entered the cover of the shrubs, the tension in her shoulders eased. Touching Dingo relieved another fear, one she couldn't name.

Messages we bring, he said to her mind. *From pack I say come away now. Danger nears.*

"And the other message?" Damasc wanted to go with him. If all her knowledge of the world was false, running with pack in the mountains she loved would be a good life. But it wasn't hers to choose while duty remained unresolved.

Look west, to the pillars of salt, speak your words and wait one day of light, one night of dark. On the dawn after thus, she speaks judgement.

"Where do I go?"

They hear. Speak.

A howl split the air, followed by two higher in the hills. Dingo lifted his head and sniffed toward the dryland forest of the foothills.

I will come should you have need.

"What are you going to say?" The boy's whisper carried clearly.

"Shhhhh. There are listeners too close, I fear." Damasc walked to the edge of the lake. Was there a pillar out there? Dingo said west. She oriented herself by the fading stars, brushed as much mud off her clothing as possible. The hair wasn't fixable. She dragged fingers through it, pushed it behind her ears. She wasn't ready. Only Mentors learned the words to seek the guidance of the Goddess. They weren't here to advise, so she'd go for her best effort.

She straightened her back and pushed out her chest. The wide expanse of salt-encrusted lakes shimmered. "I seek dispensation from the laws that sentence a child to death or sacrifice. He has the Gift. I beg the Goddess to allow me to return to Shaower to demonstrate that value. With the boy as acolyte, if possible. The Warden offers payment by blood. I offer myself in his place."

Her words disappeared into the unknowable depths of the lake.

"Is that it? Is that your petition?"

"Yes."

"Don't you think there should be more? An offering, a blessing, a word or two about their great wisdom?"

"I am a Guardian, not a Warden. I state my case plain."

"It's not like my initiation, because I must make offerings before I ask for blessing. I am expected to demonstrate knowledge of the laws of justice gifted by the Virago. You should have knelt," the boy said. "They like their petitioners to be suitably humble."

"Don't laugh at me, kid. I have never heard that lore, but . . ." Damasc snapped her mouth shut. He didn't understand. From where she stood, no path led to life. Not Shaower, where she'd be executed for failing in her duty. Nor across the salt lakes to the nomads. She was the enemy to his people. They'd kill her, as the people of Shaower killed their enemies. *The enemy is death. Death to the enemy.*

Would they let the boy live after he'd travelled with their enemy?

She turned to him. "You can return to your people if there is no answer." Let him choose his fate.

"I wouldn't make it, and I don't think you'd come with me to show me the secret to finding water, but if I have a choice, I'd like to meet whoever comes to give an answer."

"What if the answer is death?"

"Death is easy. It happens once. Life is hard, every day a struggle."

"Is that part of your teachings?" More likely his father.

"I'm hungry."

Damasc sighed and scanned the tree line for the right shade of dusty green. She pointed to a sloping beach to the south. "It's light enough. Come with me."

The ground firmed up under the swell of sand blown against the rocks. A long depression edged with whistling sheoaks.

"When was it to happen?" Damasc asked.

"What?"

"Your initiation." She walked around one tree, then another, scraped sand from around the trunk.

"The rising moon on the day of the equinox."

"You have the same ceremony days as we do?"

"We have the same Goddesses."

Did they? Was it all the same? In the teachings of the Shaower, it was One True Goddess. And in the Book of Lore, the

Goddess was referred to as the Lady of the Lake because it was where she manifested. If the lake lore was wrong, might not the rest of it be inaccurate? When was the last time anyone from Shoawer visited the lake?

Damasc showed the boy where to dig under the tree, how deep, and how to filter the mud from the water. She shared the secret of the song of the sheoaks with him, and he laughed. Her chest hurt at the sound. Her eyes smarted.

"Never steal from the same tree twice. This can kill them. Not as fast as a summer sandstorm, but if they don't drink, they die." She ruffled his hair. "Same as us."

Now for some food.

Sedges lined an area of the lakes. "Bulkuru," she said. "We can eat the roots if they're big enough."

Without a fire, they ate them raw. Tough to chew and swallow—even with a lot of water—but edible. What she'd give for a fat Bogong moth. She caught an insect, but didn't recognise it and let it go. Some risks were worth it, some were not.

What she'd learned from her mother were skills and stories, many different to the village teachings.

If the stories of the nomads were so similar to the written lore, why were they the enemy? Apart from location, what made them different? The teachings spoken to the children of Shaower felt more and more like a distant memory, or a fable. The Warden's laws condemned all who opposed her.

That was not the way of the Goddess. The stories from her mother showed the Goddess as strict, not cruel.

They set up camp at the edge of the shrubbery, overlooking the mirages that created a vision of silver water as a single entity. One lake? Maybe if the one looking was too far away to see the clusters of sedges and lumps of dirt that separated each from the others.

The sky to the east darkened. It was getting late and darker. The boy wandered to a raised mound near the lake's edge.

"What are you doing?" Damasc asked.

"I would learn my true name," he said. "I have gone three seasons unnamed. I pray for the vision to see it, for the heart and courage to accept it. It would be at the rising of the moon, but if you've already spoken to the Goddesses, I don't see why I can't." He kneeled in the mud, stared at the horizon. "Don't you have a name day ceremony?"

Damasc was an outsider because of the Gift, untested for a true name. "Those with the Gift don't undergo the Name Day ceremony. I was given the name of a weed to show my character. To warn others. If I take a true name, the Gift dies."

"I think you should meet my people. They are all named truly, and many have Gifts. Some are healer, some learn the art of fire, some are lorists, storytellers and musicians. The Gift is not without need. The newly initiated works with the elders, undertaking a promise to strengthen the gift throughout life and to mentor new acolytes." He lowered his head until it almost touched the turgid surface. Once, twice, thrice. Leaned back on his heels.

"I did not know I was gifted, except that I hid too easily from my brothers when they tormented me. I did not expect to be graced at such a late stage." He raised his head, crossed his arms over his chest. "I hoped and prayed I wasn't gifted. I wanted to become a herder." He gazed at the northern horizon. "I love the open spaces of the desert lands and did not wish to continue studies."

"Is this how you pray?"

"No, but I haven't been instructed yet, and I don't have offerings. Something happened on the way through the mountains."

"You have formal studies?"

"Of course, don't you?"

"Of course we do," she said. "We're civilised." And she'd been taught that all others were uncivilised marauders.

A raucous screech of parrots rose from the foothills to the north and east. Damasc shaded her eyes, watched and sniffed. The breeze carried salt, mud, sulphur. Nothing from the north, but a thin column of dust rose from a gully between two hills to the north and east.

Soldiers.

5.

Where was a cave, or anywhere to hide? She'd seen nothing, but what about a wombat hole? She pulled air in through her nose, rolled it over the back of her tongue, tasted for the dense fur of a cranky wombat.

Nothing. The reeds close to the water wouldn't hide them for long. No shelter in the dryland forest—the trees too widely spaced, and too spindly to climb. She squatted and touched the water, tried to raise it into a haze.

The pounding in her head stopped the attempt. This world was too wrong, too unknown. She didn't have time to learn how to shape this world to her touch.

Right now, she wanted a good hole in the ground. She scanned the area to the east and south. "We have to move."

"We're supposed to wait." The boy's voice shook. He looked toward the soldiers, turned back to the lake.

"If the Goddess . . ." Damasc couldn't finish. The Goddess would come, or not. There would be an answer one way or the other. Vrath was closer and tracking them like a starving carnivore.

The kid's face fell.

"Look for a hole, a depression. We can dig ourselves in." Were these reeds hollow? They could bury—

"What's that?" the boy pointed to the middle of the lake.

A salt eddy swirled across the surface, coming closer with each change of direction.

"Come away from the edge." Damasc pulled him into the reeds.

A piercing scream split the air. Three funnels of salt spun a frenzied dance over the water, sent sprays of sharp crystals and thick mud flying.

"Stand!"

"Who speaks?" Damasc felt her voice crack. She swallowed the lump in her throat. "If you wish us harm, I will fight." Words were all she had. "Come out, Vrath. You don't need to hide from me." Why hadn't she brought weapons?

Because she wasn't a good warrior. And a person with weapons can't climb the steep paths of the mountains.

"We wish no harm to the Guardian, nor to the one who seeks his name." The voice boomed through the air like a mountain crashing.

Damasc staggered backward. The hair on her neck sprang up like the gills of a frilled lizard. She froze inside, held her legs still, one hand on the boy. There was nobody there. No soldiers, no living creatures. The three pillars of spiralling salt spun over the lake, with no sense of life within.

"I am Guardian, and I will remove your illusions unless you show yourself." Damasc had no idea how, but they might not know the limits of her Gift.

The three pillars rose taller, spun faster, became one. A shape emerged. A tall female, dressed in white veils and flowing ethereal mists, a sword in her hand and a harness around her body.

The boy kneeled. He stretched his arms forward and lowered himself flat on the mucky ground.

"My Lady of the Virago," he whispered. "I thank you for your vision. I beg you for mercy. I seek my name."

"Arise, son of the white sands of desert and sea, and stand beside your mentor Guardian." The warrior-woman moved forward, floating over the water. Her eyes glowed like crystalline opals. "Do you see your heart-name?" She smiled, kneeled closer, whispered in his ear. "You will need this name for the task we set you." The lady leaned back again.

The boy's quaking shook the ground. Or was it Damasc shaking?

"And we must speak to your petition, Guardian."

What was the appropriate response to the Goddess? Nothing of her teaching came to mind. She bowed her head, never losing sight of the lady. "I greet you, Goddess, Lady of the Lake, and request to repeal the decision made against this boy, applied by the people of Shaower using your laws."

"Ah, we see the problem." The Goddess tilted her head. "My sisters and I agreed to hear your words, and we sought your heart in the matter. We have a question."

Wind swirled around Damasc's legs. A cold shiver slid up her back. Her feet itched to run. If she had a choice to go with the pack now, she'd take it. Too late. Her fists clenched against her thighs, her heart thumping against her ribs like a battle gong.

"State your case in terms of the laws of the just."

What and how did a petitioner present a case to the Lady of the Lake? Damasc wasn't a wordsmith, she was . . . "I am the

Guardian of the Pass. This boy was sentenced to death as an enemy. This is outside the rule of law. A child cannot be judged and condemned as an adult. I was charged with bringing him for sacrifice, but sacrifice is execution. Instead I seek the rule of law that protects children be applied." She took a shallow breath, licked her lips. "I beg that a child not be murdered in the name of false laws. I seek justice."

"Justice is a many-barbed weapon," the Lady said. "And we do not think it has been wielded well."

What did that mean? Damasc waited, mouth closed. She'd said it as it was, and feelings didn't help a legal case.

"Your appeal is for leniency in the case against your enemy?"

"A child, Goddess. I appeal on behalf of a child, one who also bears the Gift. For one to be so blessed and then executed while outside the bounds of the rule of law feels . . ." she bit her tongue, grimaced, "sacrilegious."

"Or worse."

That was what Damasc would have said, but refrained. Did the Goddess read minds?

"We read hearts, Thorn of Lore. We weigh, we measure, we judge. And we have considered your appeal."

A screaming wind blew Damasc's hair across her face. She blinked rapidly, swiped it away. Etiquette be damned. She wanted to see and remember everything.

"We have given this boy his name, and he can choose to accept or deny. Accepting a name does not deny the Gift.

Choosing matter over spirit does. However, a hard lesson is needed, and we ask more of you. A test of worthiness. Justice must prevail, and spirit comes from the courage to see truly. Therefore, we state that you will attend the village of Shaower for the Naming Day ceremony tomorrow, and you will undertake the Test of Souls. The outcome will prove that the spirit of the law is fundamental."

The Test of Souls? None returned from the test. A lesson, a warning.

"I'll do it," the boy said.

"Quiet. Let me think." Damasc stretched the tension from her shoulders. A young boy shamed her by accepting without question or fear. But he didn't know the Test of Souls, did he? She didn't, either, except that the story was a fable, a tale of terror. A reminder about what happened to those who disputed the letter of the law.

"Can he withdraw his assent if he does not know the risk? I will accept the challenge," she said, "but the boy does not need to be part of it. I request that he be allowed to return to his people." They'd called her a mentor Guardian. His Mentor. Her mind spun between the options. Live and take an acolyte. Or free him to follow his dream.

"The response is as expected. However, we have chosen. This Test of Souls requires two devotees."

"What is the benefit of this task?" Damasc had to know the purpose.

"The Test of Souls proves the heart's intent, the spirit that compels action. Success will demonstrate a value to the people who seek true justice. Failure is not something to consider. The Lore shall be rewritten and relearned by all who need to witness true sacrifice."

"The ceremony is tomorrow. At dawn. We can't get back in time."

"Leave now. Your request for a ruling from the Virago is fulfilled."

The salt-spires collapsed, became dense mirages, faded until they whooshed to nothing. Pieces of salt and stone and mud fell to the ground. A hazed sky, darkening overhead, held no warrior-shapes, sang no clarion voices.

"I say we go," the boy said. "How long to get there?" He pointed toward the lower hills.

"It's uphill, and took two days and one night to get here, so halve that time and we'd still be late."

"The pack has a different trail," he said. "A shorter path. To get ahead of the soldiers." The boy gestured toward the trail from the foothills.

"It won't be easy." Damasc knew dingo trails. If the ridgeline she'd chosen to get here was bad, the wolf tracks were worse. More dangerous than crossing a river in full snowmelt flood. And going uphill was harder than sliding down on an avalanche. Her mother's maps didn't have other choices, and either Vrath was close or she was imagining the smell of leather.

"If we don't stop, we might make it by sunrise," she said. She didn't add that it would be the day after.

6.

The light to the north changed, the horizon darkened with the dust of fast-moving soldiers sweeping toward them. Damasc pointed them out to the boy.

"We need to run." She lifted his hands and held them. "Are you ready?"

The boy nodded, his face pale.

"That way." It was the steep-sided ravine with loose shale at the far end. "We can climb up to the ridge at that point." A shadow of a deep crack meant a climbing chimney. A direct and dangerous line to the ridge. "Then we'll call the pack."

The dingoes howled, the song mournful and strident. *Come,* they called.

The boy cheered and showed her two white-tipped tails flashing near the low-lying jumble of rocks halfway up the second slope. Good eyes on the kid.

They ran single file, close to the shrubs, soft-footed and quiet. The spoor showed in the heavy soil.

Damasc ran mid-pace to cover the boy's shorter stride, spoke only to give directions. No one fooled a tracker, but soldiers weren't trackers. The foamy inlet was the turn point, and they raced around the boulders and leapt up. She looked back.

No sign of soldiers near the lake. They'd be in the shrubs. It was what she'd do.

Birds called and screeched, settled and argued. Not from disturbance, just night noises. Birds doing what birds did every night. There was neither sound nor smell of Vrath. How well did he know the region? Was his aim to cut them off somewhere?

"Keep going up." She pushed the boy's left shoulder until he turned in the right direction. "See the jagged rock? Once we're up, go there. It looks like an animal track. Low. We won't be targets against the sky."

She pushed him up the chimney rather than trust his holds, burning the muscles in her thighs and shoulders. When they squeezed from the narrow confines and moved beyond the peak, she flopped to firm ground and tapped his gourd.

"Drink," she said, licking dry lips.

The gourd swung from his waist, smashed against his hand as he turned. An arrow pierced the gourd, cracked it. Water splattered Damasc's arm. The feather of an arrow brushed her face.

The boy reached for the gourd.

"Leave it!" She pulled the boy into her arms, hefted him over her shoulder, and ran.

The stony ridge didn't have a path. No clear tracks. Too hard to carry the boy. She set him down in front to protect his back. "Run!"

The hill to the north overlooked their position. Vrath had been climbing, aiming for high ground. She should have realised.

No way down. Or back. Open to the danger from the higher vantage they had. Damasc and the boy ran low and fast, ducked behind the first rock large enough to provide cover.

"Get on my back again," she panted. The boy nodded, then wrapped his arms and legs around her. She flicked a look behind, then sprinted down a loose-filled furrow of an old avalanche, and floundered across the dangerous surface of shifting shale barely ahead of the fast-sliding rocks.

She bore down on a sheer face of stone with a dearth of cracks or handholds on the surface. But the sour sweat of men in leather wafted through the cooling air. Too close.

"Hold tight." She plunged too hard onto the escarpment, crabbed her fingers and the soft toes of the boots into hairline fractures. One grip at a time, breathing shallow, her toes cramping, fingers hot and throbbing. No time to test the holds. Once on the next ridge, the best archer didn't have a chance to make the distance.

The rock was damp. One hand slipped. Her calf screamed with the extra weight. The boy squealed and strangled her with his tightened grip. She coughed until he loosened the hold. How high were they? She looked down. Mistake. Sharp rocks that way. Damasc threw herself from hold to hold until the cliff eased into a slope. She ran on all fours and ducked over the far edge. She breathed out, let the boy's legs fall from her waist, lifted his arms from around her neck.

His head thumped onto the hard surface, his arms flopped. Blood oozed onto the rock. She rolled him. He'd been hit. The arrow in the boy's shoulder wobbled.

Damasc held her mind still, cradled his head, checked for injuries. Not much blood but still flowing. A few bruises. The tightness in her chest eased. She held the tip and squeezed the surrounding skin until the grip of the flesh eased. Not too deep. It might come out easy enough, but the bleeding needed attention. Moon-vine? She didn't have any, hadn't seen any, didn't have the time to collect it if she had. What else? She grabbed dried leaves and slid the point from the wound. Gentle, slow, firm. She compressed the leaves over the wound, pressed it down.

Dingo howled, his scent close. *Pack comes.*

"Help me." Damasc pulled the boy against her body, covered him with her coat. "I have no moon-vine." *I can't help him.*

A dark-pointed dingo crooned like a bitch with a newborn pup. *He is mine.* The bitch shuffled in, belly low to the ground, sniffed at the boy and licked his face. *Awake, pup, and do what I show.*

The boy's eyes opened. He swallowed. "She said to use the Gift."

"How? I don't have any vine or herbals." *The Lady has entrusted him to my care. I beg to share your vision.*

"As a force. Energy. A globe of light and flame. Link to me so I learn."

She lifted the compress, touched his shoulder. The boy nodded. She opened her mind as she would to Dingo, created fire with yellow flames floating above her hand. She waited for the boy's nod, then placed her palm over the oozing wound, cringed at the singe of flesh. That smell would carry far.

"Ice."

Ice was something she'd never needed. There was enough in her ordinary life. She couldn't create it.

"Push me up," he said.

When he raised his hand, it glowed snowline white. His hand was so cold it burned like frost. She helped put his hand on the burned flesh, learned from his mind-shape how to swing the request from heat to cold. The redness and swelling around the wound reduced. The boy sighed and sagged forward.

"Can you move? They're close, and we have a long way to go." Damasc hoped he'd say no, that he'd go with the pack. If the boy was too injured to go on, that was the end. The vision of the Goddess, stern and implacable, brought her out in a sweat.

"The den mother says there is another way." He scratched the ruff on the bitch's neck.

"I'm in," Damasc said. "Will she share with me?"

The den-mother's vision was strange, a movement of air like a mirage, not solid but touchable. A spark ran along the base of the vision, became a spike of lightning along the ground. The den opened into a warren of tunnels. Lying under all the pathways was something that joined them. Not like a series of caves, it was a river of emptiness that flowed in all directions. This den had a back wall that wasn't stone or earth. The vision faded. Would she have known these paths if she'd run with the pack?

"Thank you," Damasc said. The black sky flickered with pinpricks of stars that shed no light. It might help them. Even if soldiers knew the ground, they needed to see where they trod. Damasc didn't, not with Dingo sharing his night vision.

Step into the world-slip, Dingo said. *The path from here to where your memory calls.*

It wasn't far. They reached a shallow cave with a small opening. She crawled in, following the boy, and stood up. Her breath shuddered. Damasc took one step. Stopped. This was magic she didn't know or understand. Why was she doing this? To save a boy? To protect the Gift? Because the Goddess demanded it?

No.

Loyalty. Honour. Justice.

Damasc hugged the boy to her chest and ran into the empty space. She closed her eyes at the boundary between reality and something that wasn't. It was black. All black. It felt like a river, bumpy, thrown from one place to another by a flow of unstoppable snowmelt that tossed trees and rocks downstream. Her chest threatened to scream. The grip on the boy tightened.

Don't let go. Damasc closed her mouth and fled into the darkness.

7.

Bright flashes burned into the back of Damasc's eyes. She fell to the ground in a dark space, didn't feel the boy. She groped forward until she realised her eyes were closed. When she opened them, there was a gash of dark purple against the blackness. An opening. Beyond the opening the boy stood, looking up. She pushed through the thorny wild rose bushes that hid the den mouth and joined him.

They were at the base of a cliff. Broken gourds lay scattered on the ground. The trickle of water over the ledge above them was familiar. It came from the pool of water beside her hut.

Home. She breathed a prayer to the Goddess and to the pack. They still had to climb up and reach the amphitheatre before dawn. The sky tinged with red and green to the east.

Noises rattled from the cave.

"It's late. We need to hurry." Damasc lifted him onto her back and climbed the familiar cliff at a pace that would get them to the amphitheatre faster than walking the well-trod paths. After pulling them both over the cliff-face, she slid the boy off her back and they ran toward the amphitheatre, gasping. They didn't stop until Damasc lifted the mallet.

She rang the gong. Once, twice, thrice. She rested her hands on her knees, panting. The boy handed her the gourd and she slurped a mouthful between breaths. Her stomach rumbled and gurgled.

It wasn't sunrise. They were in time. The ceremonies hadn't started.

But where were the villagers? Were they coming?

If anyone other than soldiers came, and if the Chief Warden woke in time, Damasc had a message from the Goddess to impart.

The sky paled.

Footsteps pattered along the halls. People wandered in, gasped, blocked the lower tiers as they whispered and gesticulated. Still rude. The Seconds strode onto the upper tiers.

"Does a ghost ring us to order?" Their robes swished over stone as they stepped to the edge of their platform. "Begone, ghost," the Seconds chorused. "We do not deal with those who are not of the living." They shooed at Damasc.

"A ghost cannot speak, therefore, I am not a ghost. I will speak to the council before the sun rises."

"Remove her!"

Two soldiers stomped from behind the stone pillars, swords pointed at Damasc's chest. The audience buzzed.

Vrath and a handful of his soldiers surged through the open gate. He raised his sword and marched forward. "She is mine," he yelled.

Damasc raised a bubble that looked like gift-light and held it between herself and Vrath. "I have the right to call the council," she said. "This is the council that gave me a task, and I return with the message from the Goddess."

"We do not recognise you, nor your role. We have had no reports of incursions and therefore have no need for a Guardian of the Passes. You are dismissed into the care of—"

"I am here to report on the outcome of my supplication to the Goddess regarding your Chief Warden's judgement to offer this boy for sacrifice."

"Blasphemer!" both Seconds screeched. "You will be executed for speaking such evil against the Warden of our Laws."

Vrath lunged forward, sword high.

The bubble of light expanded, glowed red. Damasc moved it through the air until it was at eye level in front of Vrath. He swung his sword at it. The heat flashes and white lightning from the disc blackened the stone and set flame to the blade. He flinched and swore.

"I have a message to impart, the result of a task this council gave me." Damasc scanned the audience and returned her gaze to Vrath. "Do you wish to deny the words of the Lady of the Lake, our Goddess?"

"The Guardian will give account of herself before anyone else undertakes an ill-considered action on this ceremonial day." The Chief Warden strolled from the hall to her chair, gathered the folds of her golden robes, and sat. "However, I do think the cleansing of one's body is expected to precede such a call on the council, don't you?" She sniffed, held a cloth to her nose and gave a delicate cough.

The crowd tittered.

"Stand to, soldiers. Await orders."

Vrath bowed and sheathed his sword, but did not remove his hand from the hilt. His soldiers moved up to flank him. Blocking the gong, blocking the gate.

"The Lady has a message. She has asked that the ritual for the Test of Souls be—"

"Quiet!" The Warden slammed her staff to the floor. "You do not exist. You have broken oath, abused duty. Your rights are denied."

"I require the Test of Souls to demonstrate my words as the true spirit of the Lore."

"The Book of Laws, please." The Warden held her hand out. A Second bowed, and scuttled away.

"We don't have time to consider the writings," Damasc said. "The test must begin today, at the rising of the—"

"Yes, yes. The rising of the sun. We have time. Though there are other ceremonies to undertake today. I would suggest the Axe of Justice to your neck, but it would be inauspicious on the equinox."

A breathless Second ran into the amphitheatre. She placed the heavy book on the rolling table behind the chairs, and pushed it next to the Chief Warden.

"Here it is." A finger pressed the page.

"Does anyone know how many years since this ritual was undertaken?" The Warden ran her fingers down the page. And read from the book. "If a person requests the Test of Souls, they must be named by their true name. They must disavow their ties to Shaower, and they must prepare for a life beyond this one." Deep lines etched the face at the edge of the mask. "That means two things: you are unnamed and therefore unable to take the test, and as you are not of this village, you cannot disavow your ties." The smug voice grated through the mask.

Silence filled the amphitheatre.

Damasc felt herself shrivel. This was impossible. How did the Goddess not know of these strictures? Could Damasc name herself on this day and say it was her true name? Lie? No. She'd trust the Goddess and the boy.

The Warden raised a finger to the chin of the mask. "I have the right to refuse the request, based on the needs of the people, and the purpose of the quest. Therefore, I deny your request."

The boy stepped forward. "I seek to undertake the Test of Souls with my Mentor," he said. "The request of one is an offer, the request of two is irrefutable. Read the words on the page, and if any words are false, condemnation to the one who misspeaks."

Damasc smiled. The kid had a way with fancy words. Even if he was guessing or had the Goddess in his ear, he better be right.

"What is this? Remove it, immediately." The Warden stamped her foot and slammed the staff on the ground.

Vrath lifted his sword.

"No!" Damasc pulled the boy close, made another bubble of red flame in her other hand. "The Goddess has chosen this boy. Is that not enough? Why do you risk the protection of the Lady by going against her wishes? Hear what I say, listen to her words."

"You do not speak for the Goddess." The Second raised her staff like a spear, aimed it at Damasc.

The arena before the petitioner's block swirled with dirt and stones. Salt stung Damasc's eyes. She squinted, stood her ground. Cyclonic winds tore at clothing, knocked soldiers to the ground. The gong boomed and rattled in its frame. Robes and wigs flew. People screamed and fell from their seats, held each other and cried out.

One pillar flung upward like a new mountain, white at the highest peak, dark as tannin where it touched the quaking ground. Another pillar roared like an avalanche, slid and compressed and braided with the first. Snow and Stone. A white opal shimmer cut the light like a well-honed knife blade as the third pillar emerged. The three pillars joined, folded into each other, became more. Eyes glowed, mouth opened, hair floated.

The spinning stopped. The vision solidified. The ground stilled, the rumble of stones settled.

"Read it, Warden of false words." The Lady towered above the tier of the Warden and her Seconds.

The crowd gasped. Every head dropped low, every knee touched the ground. A hundred soldiers emerged from behind pillars and prostrated themselves.

"Justice is not false words, but truth and deeds. We are here to represent justice, and to ensure our words are heard with clarity." She rose again, until she was three times higher than the Warden's tier. The Lady's translucence highlighted the changing hues of the sky. "Are there any who wish to dispute our words?"

Silence plunged the halls and tiers into a stillness without breath.

"We have chosen our representatives to undertake the Test of Souls." The Lady smiled at Damasc and the boy. "Not as a consequence of their lack. They have agreed to test in order to redeem the people of this village, those who have lost their understanding of the words within the Book of Lore. We have heard voices deny that choice, and our message." She gazed over the tiers, and the backs of the soldiers. "Perhaps we need to choose new representatives from among you. Is your soul prepared? Will you survive beyond the first plunge into the bitter cold of truth?" She snapped her fingers.

The audience jumped, their pale faces raised, hands and mouths pleading as tears rolled down their faces.

"They choose to test for those who deny that the Book of Our Lore is not this book." The Lady raised the book from the hands of the Warden and dropped it to the ground. It shattered into shards and splinters.

"The book of lies is gone, and the words within are no more. Bring me your Book of Lore that we may judge the words within as our own."

No one moved.

"Now, or dust is what will remain of your village."

The Seconds backed away, heads bowed to waist height.

"The Test of Souls will commence with the naming of the Guardian. She will give her true name now, so it may be written into the teachings."

Damascena scratched at the bloody mark on her wrist, made by the thorns outside the cave near her hut. The name they'd given her in jest felt right. She was prickly, tough, useful. The scent wafted under her nose. She loved that smell, the taste of the hips.

"Damascena, Thorn of Lore, Guardian and Mentor," Damasc's words rose from deep within her soul. A weight lifted from her body, from her mind. Her heart beat strong and she grinned so wide it hurt her jaw.

"And you?" The Lady turned to the boy.

"I am Cidingo," he said. "Cub of mountain dog spirit."

"I ask you both: are you willing to pass beyond this life to undertake this pilgrimage that is a Test for your Soul?"

"I am," Damasc and Cidingo said at the same time.

The Lady reduced her size and sat down next to the Warden. "They are taking such a long time to return, are they not? Please call them back."

The Warden froze, mouth open. It didn't last long. "This is inappropriate. I am the law in this village. I am the Chief Warden." She lifted her staff. "Soldiers! Guards!"

"You have punished and enslaved, you have ruled with hatred and division. That is not law, not as spoken to the people who begged us for mercy when they arrived here." The face of the Goddess darkened like a raging storm, the chill of her breath formed icicles on the chairs of law. "Is it?" Her hands clenched into fists as she blasted the cold glare around the amphitheatre.

The crowd made a strange noise, like a person strangled, unable to breathe.

"Have you forgotten our teachings? After a hundred years with no contact, do our words remain in your books? Do we fail to exist if you do not believe? Do you not know that we see all, hear all, remember all? We live in a plane above and beyond this world, bound to earth and air and sea. We gave freedom and simple rules, and a Book of Lore for guidance." She clapped her hands and blasted a salty wind across the tiers. "With that freedom comes responsibility, aided by laws. We have three unbreakable rules for those who wish to abide."

One finger extended from her hand.

"The rules of law are for the good of all, and apply to all.

"Loyalty is to the rule of law, not to those who administer.

"External expression must reflect internal truths."

The Lady scratched the stone wall, created a set of scales. "We are the Warriors of the Word. How do we ensure the words are true? A demonstration is in order, so none forget."

The gong rang three times in rapid succession. The mallet that rested against Damasc's leg resonated with the gong, although she had neither raised it, nor rung it.

The Goddess laid her hands beside the scales. "I call this council to order. The agenda is simple. The Warden and her Seconds are decried as criminals. The people of Shaower will vote a new council into effect this day. There will be no slaves, no indentured, no executions. Justice will prevail, or dust."

The Chief Warden slunk from her chair, shoulders sagging. The Seconds were gone, slipped away when they had the chance. Vrath offered his arm to the Warden.

The Lady whirled, her shape changing too fast to see. When the air calmed, her attire was different. It was sheer, gossamer white from floating hair to frothy hem, and a new harness on her back bearing two swords. Her hands held two knives studded with opals the colour of a stormy sunset.

"Justice demands recompense," she said. "Shall I remove your wealth, your home, or your head?"

The Warden screamed and ran down the hall, throwing her mask and robe to the ground. Vrath pushed past the immobile soldiers, lifted the Warden over his shoulder. One leg froze to stillness in mid-air. His body floated off the ground, and he swung until the Warden faced the Lady again.

"No," the Lady said. "There will be no death. We do not break our laws, but there are consequences for those who subvert, squander or subjugate the power of our edicts."

The villagers groaned and lowered their faces, covered themselves with robes and shawls.

"What does the Thorn of Lore have to say?"

"The Lost Souls," Damasc said. Maybe the Warden would meet people she'd judged harshly.

"The Warden will be taken to the Lake of Lost Souls to beg mercy from all those who came to an end before their time, by her words."

The Warden squealed.

Vrath fell from the air with a thud, dropped the Warden. He double-gripped his sword, growled, used it like a staff to hold himself upright.

"The one who chooses to guard the Warden shall accompany his mother until she repents."

"I object," Vrath pulled one hand from his sword, ruined the attempted salute with a shaking hand.

"Do not delay. There is no discussion. You undertook her orders to the point of obsession, gained rank through the use of pain and force, and your family connections. This is your test, also. Be her guide until the souls are satisfied of her change." The Goddess leaned in close to Vrath, her hair flying like knives around her head. Her eyes flashed red. The light reflected from Vrath, and his skin blistered.

The sword fell to the ground with a clatter. Vrath lifted the Warden from the floor, turned his back on the Lady, and strode away. The Warden screeched until Vrath gagged her.

"The spirit of the Lore, and all laws that come from the Lore, is for the higher purpose, for the rights of all who seek justice." The Lady turned her attention to Cidingo and Damasc. "The Test of Souls remains. Before you enter into the spirit of the Lore, you must undertake to commit to the task, to make oath to undertake the role of Guardians of the Lore."

The silence hung in the amphitheatre like a snowed-in night.

"Do you sacrifice your life to die separated from all those who were part of it?"

Damasc nodded and Cidingo grinned and said, "Yes!"

"Do you sacrifice every breath of your life to seek the truth of Lore?"

They looked at each other, smiled, and kept nodding. "I do!" they both said.

The Lady flourished her hands through the air, shaped a slice of time and space to the entrance of the ceremonial cave.

The new moon rose over the horizon, a bright blue-white omen for the new season on the day of the equinox. The rising sun lit up the same symbol on the Lady's clasp.

"This is a day equal in the blessings of day and night, as written in the Book of Lore."

The ground in front of Damasc darkened, blackened, emptied of stone. A set of rough-hewn steps led down. She turned to Cidingo, the question in the tilt of her head. He nodded. Damasc held her hand out to him, he took it, laughing, and they entered the darkness, the void of unknowing.

The last words Damasc heard before the amphitheatre closed behind her was the Lady, the Virago, the Goddess.

"Council is dismissed. For now. Duty to the law is duty to justice. Do not deny our word, or we shall return as the true Warriors, to enact the final word and close your book."

8.

The cave mouth opened onto a vista of wide blue. Fresh salt air breezed through the opening.

"It's so big," Damasc whispered, her body trembling at the strangeness of the too-wide, too-empty, too-open stretch of water with no land on the horizon.

"This is where it all begins," Cidingo said. "The ocean."

"What happened? What will happen?"

"I'll teach you how to fish, and you teach me how to harvest water."

"I mean, what happened to the people?"

He shrugged. "We did good. We live. We give thanks. And we follow the Lore."

Damasc stared at the ocean. "What are we supposed to do?"

"Listen," Cidingo said.

Two dingoes howled, one voice answering the other.

"They're here?"

"We walked their trail."

"What's that?" Damasc shaded her eyes and squinted at the strange shape on the horizon.

"That's danger. Pirates or slavers."

"The Lady doesn't like slavery."

"She said that." Cidingo smiled and cracked his knuckles.

"I thought you wanted to be a herder."

"Yes, but which animals would tolerate the smell of one who dens with dingoes?" He scowled. "When I think on it, you captured me, the pack saved me, the Goddess threw me into a new world. We're here for a reason." He pointed at the sails of two more ships that rounded the headland. "Our purpose is not ended with one test."

"Let's go," Damasc said, and moved out of the cave and into a new life. "And you can tell me the stories of the nomads."

"We are the Yarayama, the screaming wings of ocean and desert."

About the Author:

Cage Dunn is a Fibber, Fabricator, Teller of Tall Tales. It's true. Cage has lived all over Australia, now in Adelaide. Worked at everything from sewage collection to computing, eventually graduated with a BA Comm (Prof. Writing) and a Grad Dip Computing. Still learning, still writing . . .

Find Cage at:
https://cagedunn.wordpress.com/
https://www.bookbub.com/authors/cage-dunn Twitter @cage_dunn and many other places.

This is the Dawning

(Part X)

Helena McAuley

Thálassélas.

The word rebounds through my skull, pulling at memories, reshaping thoughts.

Thálassélas . . .

What did it mean?

I feel I should know.

I don't.

Douglas and Virgo speak of meaningless things. I let them. Virgo, always so affable, always able to charm. And Douglas, so willing to be charmed. I don't care for their chatter, my eyes dart around the small room, watching each corner, feeling a presence, sensing a *threat.*

But there is nothing here. And besides, my attention is elsewhere.

Thálassélas . . .

The word feels old, carries with it the weight of time, sorrow, and the smell of the ocean. Smells are supposed to draw forth memory, but this is operating in reverse. I don't know *how*, only that it is. I don't wish to admit it, even to myself, but that this word means something, something I cannot recall, troubles me. The weight of millennia has never felt so heavy, my mind has never been stretched so thin. I can recall every day—every moment—of this incarnation, but not a single moment before.

My lives have been lost to me.

I have become *this* Capricorn. Not an ageless monument to my fundamental nature, but a man.

I remember every day . . .

But even that isn't true, is it?

I do not remember who I was when this life began.

Douglas is speaking to me. I can barely hear his voice.

"Pardon?" I ask.

"Virgo says he's going to come with us, and I told him it's alright. Kay?"

I frown. "Come with us to where?"

"To see Libra."

The name brings me, body and mind, to stillness. I did not intend to visit Libra. But the Dawning is nearly upon us, I can sense it in the yearning of the earth, in the electricity of the air, the impatience of billions of minds. I can sense it in Douglas; in the part of him that is still human—even if he is unaware of it. Allies are still needed. The war is not yet won.

I exhale in futile deliberation. My hand, it seems, has been forced. "Fine."

The train ride is not long. Nor is the walk to Libra's home. Yes, I know where Libra is—I will always know where Libra is. The apartments and flats surrounding the station give way to more established houses, which then melt into larger, modern homes.

As we walk, Virgo gives a low whistle. "Libra has some money this time around," he says.

I do not reply.

The house before which I stop is large; double story, all concrete and glass, pillared entrance. Inside, children are shrieking with joy. I cannot avoid my hesitation. To undo centuries of cultivated inaction is a step my body is unwilling to take. And yet, have I not always been master of this body? Surely my mind is strong enough to override its wants and desires. Surely, I still have that strength.

Virgo's voice is soft and compassionate as he speaks. "How long has it been since you've seen Libra?"

Seen? Or interacted? I answer for the latter. "Nine hundred years, give or take."

"Why?" Douglas pauses. "What's wrong with Libra?"

I take a deep breath. "There is nothing wrong with Libra." And I ascend the stairs.

The bell chimes, the children inside react with excitement. Footsteps approach, patient cajoling, a tired sigh. The door opens, and there is Libra.

Of course she's a woman. Libra has eschewed the masculine form. Ever since—

This incarnation is in its fourth decade, and she has aged well. Homely but beautiful, strong, determined. Eyes of striking hazel, long hair of shining blond, without the touch of the grey mark.

Virgo's anxious voice sounds, loud enough to pierce all our minds. *She's not incarnate!*

The hazel eyes fix me with a baleful stare.

"Yes, she is," I say.

Libra closes the door behind her and her eyes flicker over my companions. "Virgo." She acknowledges him with a nod of her head before turning to Douglas. "Human," she greets him. Then she turns to me. "What the hell do *you* want?"

"It is the Dawning," I state.

"Not yet, it isn't," she bites back. "The world is in preparation, but the Dawning hasn't started. And how *dare* you try to recruit me like some lackey. I thought you had more sense than that, but I perpetually overestimate you."

I deserve that.

"Aquarius needs allies." I keep my tone even.

Her arms fold across her chest. "Then Aquarius can ask me in person, but my answer will still be the same."

"Err, hi," Douglas speaks. He shrinks from the conflict but raises a hand. "Wanna be my ally? We're doing a sort of PUG thing."

"I have no idea what you're talking about," Libra snaps.

"'Pick Up Group'?" Muttering he adds, "I thought it was obvious."

His attempt at humour does nothing to cool Libra's ire. "No," she growls. "I don't care. I'm not a soldier—not this time around. And I am *not* risking this incarnation. I am a *wife* and I am a *mother*, and that is *exactly* what I want to be. The Dawning can hang itself; *you* can hang yourself. And *you*"—she turns her eyes back to me, her finger rising to strike me in the chest—"*you* can die screaming, for all I care."

She throws open the door, but stops and turns. "It was lovely to see you again, Virgo. If you manage to survive you should stop by for tea sometime."

"And you can give me the name of your hairdresser." Virgo winks back.

Libra throws me one last hate-filled glance.

My face is impassive. What do I feel? Anger? Resentment? Guilt? I do not know. The fault was hers; and it was mine. Part of me wants to grasp her and scream, part of me wants to hear her forgiveness. Most of me does not want her to turn away. Still, I let her go.

Douglas does not. "Hang on, wait! You can't just leave like this!"

"And why the hell not?"

He steps forward. "Look, I only found out about all this stuff yesterday. Since then, I've been beaten up, shot with mythic lasers, nearly drowned in zombies, and work hasn't even called to see why I didn't show up this morning." He speaks as if the last is the greatest of his troubles. "And, yeah, all of that is *his* fault." He levels a finger at me. "Now, I don't know what Cap did to piss you off, but I can imagine. I mean, he's a stubborn prick—"

I frown at that.

"—and politeness isn't in his vocabulary—"

My frown becomes a glare.

"—but he's got everyone's best intentions at heart, and that's got to be worth something. So if I can stand by him after all he's put me through, the lease you can do is hear him out."

I'm shocked by Douglas' words. Not because of his somewhat counterintuitive endorsement of me, but because of what I hear in his voice.

Love.

Libra has heard it, too. She looks him up and down. "Watch him," she says bitterly. "You'd be just his *type*."

The words confuse Douglas, but they set my teeth on edge. "That was four of your incarnations ago," I growl. "And I've *told* you, it wasn't about your body; it was about *who you were*."

"Yeah, right," Libra scoffs. "Tell me you're not just afraid of *breasts*." And she grabs at the appendages to illustrate her point.

"I'm not," I say. "I loved you, Libra."

Douglas is shocked by my statement, Virgo is trying to be as unassuming as possible, but my gaze is fixed on Libra. Fixed on the narrowing of her eyes, the wrathful curl of her lips, the lift of her chest as she draws breath.

"Go to hell," she spits, and slams the door behind her.

Damn her! My neck tightens and my hands curl into fists. I cannot supress the growl that escapes me.

Douglas baulks. "Cap, don't—!"

But I am already unmanifest. Already moving through the door.

Libra's home is beautiful without being ostentatious. Just like her; everything in balance. Almost everything. But I don't care for the tasteful throws or long hallway lined with family photos. I move unmanifest through the house, ignoring the children and their toys, ignoring the walls in my path, seeking only her.

She is in the kitchen. It is large, clean, warm. Marble and wood contrasting and complimenting. She's leaning on an island bench, head bowed into her hands and a half-finished coffee before her. I wait. I watch. Unnoticed. As I have done so many times before. Now, as always, I am touched with longing, and touched with anger.

I have not seen this incarnation in many years, but I remember when I first saw it. She was a child, no older than those now in her care. I kept my distance, as I always do, but I knew what was coming. It was what had drawn me to her. The child was happy, lost in a world of her imagination, dolls in her hands and horses braying in the adjoining paddock. Then she incarnated. I could feel as well as hear the screams. I watched her collapse to the ground, and then rise with the weight of lifetimes on her shoulders.

I remember watching as the hazel eyes turned grave, as the light of innocence was snuffed out and she was a child no longer.

I remember a time, much earlier, when Libra was mine. And I remember the moment I lost him.

She sniffs and raises her head, running both hands through her hair. Her eyes are reddened, but not wet. Still, it seems that tears had not been far away.

She looks at me, despite my lack of physical form.

"For god's sake," she berates me like I'm one of her children. "Capricorn, manifest. Now."

I oblige.

"You never did know when to leave well enough alone," she mutters, turning on the kettle and preparing a mug for coffee.

I lower myself onto a stool at the bench. "I've left you alone for centuries."

She snorts. "No you haven't. You sneak around and you stalk and you tinker and you make sure everything is going along according to your little plan." The mockery drips from her as she passes me the coffee. "Don't think I haven't noticed you. I just won't let *you* get to *me* anymore. I've moved on, Capricorn. It's time you did the same."

I cannot stop my muscles from tensing. I cannot stop the bitterness in my voice as I speak. "You move on quickly, Libra."

"Nine centuries, Capricorn," she snaps. "I wouldn't call that 'quick'. And remember, *you* rejected *me*."

"You dis-incarnated."

"I was tired!" she shouts, bashing the flat of her hand on the bench. "I'm not like you, Capricorn! I *can't* be human century after century. What did you want me to do? Remain like that for millennia? Wear the same form until it overtook me and immured me to the physical realm? I loved you, but I had to rest!"

"I loved you, too."

"Did you? Or did you love *him*? Did you love me, or my incarnation?"

"What does it matter?" and the venom exhales in my breath. "You dis-incarnated. You left me, without even *telling* me. Two centuries I mourned the loss of you."

"And then I came back, and you wouldn't have me," she growls, her tone low and full of threat. "For years I begged you to dis-incarnate with me, Capricorn."

"I could not do that."

"We were nowhere *near* a Dawning!" her fist pounds the bench again. "The world would've turned just fine without you for a few hundred years, but staying would have been death for me. I couldn't remain here without losing my *self.* You have no idea how hard it is for the rest of us to remain in one form! You make it look easy!" She reaches across the island bench and grasps my hand. "I respect you enormously for what you've been able to do, but you have to see that it's not natural for the rest of us. You've maintained yourself for thousands of years, and I have no idea how you've managed it. But you can't hold it against me just because I couldn't do what you have done."

She pauses, inviting me to respond. *Pleading* with me to respond. Yet the words do not come to my mind. Except one:

Thálassélas.

Slowly, wary realisation comes to her. First to her eyes, and then to the muscles of her face. She retracts her hands and leans back; scrutinising me.

"My god," she breathes. "You haven't, have you?"

Guilt tightens my jaw, stills my breath, steals my voice. I look away from her; shame a bond tight about my chest. She knows. Once, she knew me in a way none other of the Twelve ever could have, and the centuries have not diluted her understanding. Libra can *see me.* She knows what I once was, and what I am now, and how the two are no longer conjoined.

"You've forgotten yourself."

My voice is a bitter rasp. "I have."

"You need to dis-incarnate."

Determination flares within me, shattering the pressing crush of guilt and shame. "No," I tell her. "I cannot. I may have forgotten myself, but I have not forgotten the plan. The order. I will do what needs to be done."

She sighs, her body once more folding towards the bench. "Sometimes I think your stubbornness will be the death of us all." Her eyes seek mine again. "Just promise me, once the Dawning has passed and the Age of Aquarius begins, dis-incarnate. Rest. Take the time to become whole again."

I do not answer.

"Capricorn, please," she pleads. "Promise me."

"I will not make a promise I may not be able to keep."

Frustration seizes her limbs. Her teeth grit and a ragged breath escapes her. "Foolish goat," she derides.

A scream from the playroom draws our attention, but it is quickly followed by laughter that puts Libra at ease.

"Do they know?" I ask her. "That they are adopted?"

"Of course." Her eyes linger on the walls that separate us from her children. "They know mummy can't have babies. We tell them they were born from my heart, not my womb." Her gaze slides back to mine. "I am very happy in this life, Capricorn. I know it may look mundane from the outside, but this life is very precious to me."

"Then your best chance to keep it is to side with us at the Dawning," I tell her.

She shakes her head. "No, Capricorn."

"Libra, you know what future your children will face in an Age of Sagittarius—"

"I will not attend the Dawning."

The statement pulls me up short. The Dawning is a compulsion that none of the Twelve can ignore. It is the one time in all of our existence that we are utterly subject to the will of the universe. It is almost a contract; we have full reign, full discretion, against the laws of reality, if we but bend to this one act of will. I cannot believe her words, and yet the ferocity in her voice, the unbending dissidence in her eyes, causes me to entertain that it is possible.

"How?" I ask.

She opens a draw, takes out a white pharmaceutical box, and places it on the bench between us. I do not require doctors. I do not fall sick. I have no idea what this is.

"A sleeping drug," she says to my uncomprehending expression. "At the first inkling of the Dawning I'm taking the whole goddamned box."

"Libra, won't that kill your incarnation?"

She shakes her head. "This body will fight to stay alive. It will fight to be at the Dawning. I've already told my husband as much as he needs to know. He'll keep an eye on me, call an ambulance if needed. But I think this will incapacitate me for at least six hours, maybe as much as nine if I'm lucky. It should be enough."

"Libra—"

"Don't," she cuts me off, but her tone is tender. "Capricorn, please don't. You know I would maintain the order, but I can't risk the battle. I can't risk this life. I can't risk leaving my children without a mother. Please." She reaches across the bench and gasps my hand again, the white box a barrier between us. "Let me have this."

Her eyes bore into mine, a well of pleading tinged with fire. Her hand feels warm, feels secure, feels *right*. I am filled with bodily urgings; to embrace her, to press my lips to hers, to enwrap my fingers with her hair. But that life has passed us, and this cold reality has taken its place. She is happy in this life, and I am beginning to realise how futile my millennia of existence has been.

Can I allow her to escape the Dawning? Can the war be won without each and every soldier?

My eyes harden. I make my decision.

Doug's eyes remained fixed on the door to Libra's home, a disquieted fidgeting to his bearing and his mind awhirl. What the hell was Capricorn *doing* in there? Should he stay? Should he go? What if Libra had already sided with Sagittarius? Would Capricorn attack her outright, as he did Cancer? Doug had no doubt that Libra would be able to defend herself, but there were children in there!

"Calm down, Doug," Virgo's melodic voice broke through the haze of indecision. "They're just rehashing the past." He sat on the steps, working a file over his nails and inspecting his progress at intervals. "This is probably the first time they've talked since 'the incident'. It will be good for them. Although Cap will most likely send Libra running straight into Sagittarius' arms." Virgo laughed at the prospect.

Doug released a frustrated breath, but he turned away from the door. He stared at the pavement before them, a tension in his muscles he was unused to. Yesterday, when Capricorn had arrived at his door, he'd felt terror, and then a juvenile excitement—as if his years of hoping and yearning for something more to this life had come to fruition. But after Mia, and Cancer, and this morning in Pisces' garden . . . He was beginning to realise the severity of this undertaking. How childishly he'd shrugged off Capricorn's assessment that this was a *war*.

But a war for what, exactly?

"Elham?"—Virgo met the name with an inquisitory hum— "What would happen if . . ." Doug hesitated. He cleared his throat. "What would happen if Sagittarius won?"

The file stilled, and Virgo lifted his eyes to the sky. He shrugged. "Then she would rule the next Age."

"But what would that mean?"

"Well, for a start, Libra wouldn't have such a nice house."

Doug sighed, his shoulders sagging.

"Has Capricorn explained to you about spiritual versus material growth?" Virgo asked.

"A little," Doug admitted. "He said that Aquarius will unite the two."

Virgo looked at him. "Do you believe that?"

With a wretched noise, Doug bent his head between his knees, cupping it with his hands. "I don't know," he moaned. "I'm just *me*. How am I supposed to do anything like that?"

"By just being you." Doug turned his head, and Virgo was smiling, face shining with adoration and love. "There's nothing you need to *do*; you just need to *be*. The Aquarian nature will infiltrate every fibre of existence. That's just how it works. Nothing will happen immediately; you need to remember that an Age is quite a long time for humans. Let me ask you, have you ever dreamt of exploring the stars?"

"Only about fifty times a week since I was six."

"Good. Under the influence of Aquarius, that's a real possibility, now that humanity has come as far as it has."

Doug processed that statement, then slowly raised his head.

"So, in an Age of Aquarius, humans will be living a Star Trek?"

Virgo shrugged. "By the end of it, maybe." He took a breath, as if searching for the right words. "The dreams you have, your hopeful belief in the possibilities for the future, your desire for *more*, these don't just come from Doug—they're part of Aquarius. It is *your nature*. Under your guidance, those same hopeful dreams will infect all of humanity. You don't need to do anything expect be who you have always been."

Virgo's words were reassuring, yet still Doug was tinged with doubt.

"But couldn't it all go wrong?"

Virgo hesitated.

"I mean," Doug pressed, "if that's what Aquarius *does*, and Aquarius has had Ages before, why is humanity in the state it's in? Why are things so messed up?"

"Well . . ." Virgo's lips pressed into a thin line. "Humanity has to be made ready, too. They have to be ready to accept their fate. Each Age has its own balance of spirituality and materialism. Some have a little more of *this* and some a little more of *that*. Humanity needs to learn to carry the balance with them as they progress. If they don't, then . . ."

Doug finished for him, "If they don't, then it can lead to their destruction."

Virgo stared at him; the gentle curve of his lips again marred into a bloodless line. Virgo nodded.

Doug huffed a breath. It was beginning to make sense. "Too much of the spirit, and civilisation crumbles. Too much of the material, and humanity will destroy itself. Aquarius is a great expansion in both, but humanity needs to 'carry the balance with them'. If the groundwork isn't laid . . ."

Virgo smiled again; beneficent and pitying. "I think you're starting to remember."

"Yeah." Doug's laugh was bitter. *But remember what?* He turned his head towards him again. "What about Sagittarius?" he asked. "What's her balance?"

Virgo laughed. "She doesn't have one."

Doug frowned and opened his mouth to ask more, but as he did, Capricorn manifest between them and strode down the steps and out onto the path. After a shocked moment, Doug and Virgo followed.

"What happened?" Doug asked.

"Will Libra side with us?" Virgo asked with equal urgency.

"No," Capricorn said, but did not slow.

Virgo let out a deeply held breath, furrowed brow smoothing as he gave a bright smile. "Don't be too hard on yourself, Cap. Sagittarius can be very persuasive when she wishes to be."

"Libra will not side with Sagittarius, either," Capricorn replied. "She will not be at the Dawning."

"What?" Virgo pulled short in his stride.

Doug hastened to catch up with Capricorn. "What do you mean she 'won't be at the Dawning'?" he asked. "What does that even mean?"

"We have to go back!" Virgo called. "She *has* to be there!"

Capricorn stopped and turned, giving Virgo an irritated glance and dismissing him. "She has found a way to avoid the Dawning," he explained to Doug. "And I am allowing her."

"Allowing?" Doug said. "What? Are you her keeper, now? Hang on, can she even *do* that?"

"Capricorn! We have to go back!"

"I'm not certain her method will work," Capricorn continued, "but I believe she has earnt the opportunity to try."

Doug's hands balled into fists in irritation. "Geez, Cap, can you pick a channel and stick with it? You try to kill Cancer because she doesn't go along with you; you won't shut up about how Sagittarius is the biggest threat humanity has ever seen; you try to kill me because 'better you than them'; and then you up and don't care about Libra because, what? Because she had sex with you? A bit of damn consistency would be nice!"

"Do not speak of things you know nothing about," Capricorn growled, teeth bared.

"Then *explain it* to me!" Doug snapped.

"Capricorn—"

It was the meekness, the frozen grip of fear rich in Virgo's voice, that made them turn.

A man held Virgo in a lover's embrace. Doug recoiled at the scared arms that held Virgo immobilised, the bloodied knuckles that grasped tight. It was the embrace of a lover turned possessive with hate, and as Doug caught the dark rimmed eyes that peered past Virgo's bloodless face, his own blood chilled.

"Scorpio," Capricorn breathed.

The smile that lit the man's face was feral.

"An eye for an eye, Capricorn," he hissed.

Virgo did not even have the time to scream as Scorpio tore him apart.

THIS IS THE DAWNING (PART X)

To be continued in the next edition of the Zodiac Series—
Scorpio . . .

About the Author:

Helena McAuley has always aspired to be a writer, except for a brief time in 1994 when she wanted to be a pair of scissors, but she couldn't cut it. As matters stand, she continues to be 'aspirational'.

She has a deep and abiding love for commas.

This is the Dawning *is a serialised debut that will be published throughout the ASF Zodiac series. We said this would end in trouble. But what can Cap and Doug do against Scorpio? Find out in the next anthology!*

Helena can be found (mostly) twit-ing, (sometimes) insta-ing, and is (rarely) facebookified under the handle @thathmc

A libratorian must always seek balance. A libatorian must always seek whisky.

ABOUT AUSSIE SPECULATIVE FICTION

Aussie Speculative Fiction is a recently established group which was created to support and promote Australian speculative fiction writers.

Check out our links:

www.facebook.com/Aussiespeculativefiction/

www.twitter.com/aussiefiction

www.aussiespeculativefiction.com

www.books2read.com/rl/asf

ABOUT DEADSET PRESS

Deadset Press is the publishing imprint of Aussie Speculative Fiction—a community aimed at supporting Australian and Kiwi authors. You can learn more at:

www.aussiespeculativefiction.com

ALSO BY DEADSET PRESS

Gemini (The Zodiac Series #6)

Cancer (The Zodiac Series #7)

Leo (The Zodiac Series #8)

Virgo (The Zodiac Series #9)

Libra (The Zodiac Series #10)

Scorpio (The Zodiac Series #11)

Sagittarius (The Zodiac Series #12)